THE KINGFISHER TREASURY OF

Ballet
Stories

KINGFISHER
a Houghton Mifflin Company imprint
222 Berkeley Street
Boston, Massachusetts 02116
www.houghtonmifflinbooks.com

First published in 1998
4 6 8 10 9 7 5 3
3TR/1204/THOM/MA/115IWF

LIBRARY OF CONGRESS CATALOGING-IN-PUBLICATION DATA
The Kingfisher treasury of ballet stories / chosen by Caroline Plaisted.
p. cm
Summary: A collection of ballet stories featuring such authors as
Bel Mooney, Noel Streatfeild, and Margaret Mahy.
1. Ballet—Juvenile Fiction. 2. Children's Stories. [1. Ballet—
Fiction. 2. Short Stories.] I. Plaisted, Caroline.
PZ5.T7445   1998   [Fic]—dc21
97-32276 CIP AC

ISBN 0-7534-5630-3
ISBN 978-07534-5630-9

Printed in India

THE KINGFISHER TREASURY OF

Ballet Stories

CHOSEN BY CAROLINE PLAISTED
ILLUSTRATED BY PATRICE AGGS

KINGFISHER
BOSTON

CONTENTS

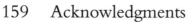

SILVER SHOES

Jean Ure

It was Charlotte's birthday, and one of her presents was a beautiful new pair of ballet shoes. Bright silver! She had never had silver ballet shoes before. They had always been boring old pink.

"Aren't they gorgeous?" said her mom. "I got them specially for your end-of-year show!"

Charlie's ballet school always put on a show at the end of the year. This year it was *The Parrot's Party*. All the birds of the air were coming to the parrot's party. Thrushes and sparrows, robins and jays, blue tits and larks—just every kind of bird you could think of. Charlie was going to be a peacock!

"I asked Miss Hillary," said Mom. Miss Hillary was Charlie's dancing teacher. "She said that silver would go nicely with your costume."

"Yes," Charlotte nodded. She brushed her cheek against the satiny smoothness of the shoes. Silver *would* go with her costume.

"Don't you want to try them on?" said Mom.

Charlie's mom was really excited that Charlie was going to be in the end-of-year show. Far more excited than Charlie was!

What Charlie loved best were the silver shoes.

They fitted perfectly! Mom had even sewn on the elastic, as it was Charlie's birthday. That was good! Charlie hated sewing.

"Can I take them to school?" she said.

Her mom hesitated.

"To show people? Please, Mom!"

"Well . . . all right! You can take them," said her mom. "But mind you don't get them dirty! You've got to wear them for the show."

"I'll take *really* good care of them," promised Charlie.

She carried them to school all wrapped up in tissue paper, in her school bag. At breaktime she showed them to her friends.

"Oh!" said Nicole. "They're silver!"

"For my show," said Charlie.

"They're lovely," said Janine.

"Really lovely," agreed Susila.

"You mustn't touch!" Charlie slid both her hands inside the shoes and held them high above her head. She did a little twirl, showing them off.

Janine, Nicole, and Susila stared admiringly at the beautiful ballet shoes.

"When is the show?" said Nicole.

"Saturday, 15th July," said Charlie; and she pulled a little face as if she wasn't too terribly thrilled about it.

"That's the day of Christopher's party!"

"Yes, I know," said Charlie.

"You won't be able to go!"

"*I know*," said Charlie.

Christopher Carr was the handsomest boy in all the class. He hadn't invited many girls to his party. Just Charlie and her friends. And now she couldn't go!

"Well, I suppose the show is more important than a party," said Susila.

"Mm," said Charlie. "I suppose." She didn't sound too certain.

The truth was, Charlie Osborne didn't particularly

care whether she was in the show. She had a little solo all of her own, when she got to wear a beautiful blue dress with a short, frilly skirt, and a bird mask made of feathers—and, of course, the new silver shoes. It would be fun to dress up and fun to see her name in the program and to hear all the people clapping. But if she hadn't been chosen, she wouldn't really have minded.

Charlie only went to ballet classes to please her mom. When her mom had been Charlie's age, she had wanted to be a ballet dancer more than anything else in the world! But it wasn't what Charlie wanted. Charlie wanted to be an airline pilot—or a policewoman—or a deep-sea diver.

What she most definitely didn't want to be was a ballet dancer !

She loved her silver shoes and she loved showing them to her friends; but she would have loved it even more if she could have gone to Christopher's party. She hated the thought of the others being there, and not her.

"Hey!" Janine gave her a nudge. "There's someone else trying to look at your shoes!"

Charlie turned, and saw Lally Richards craning her neck.

"What's she think she's doing?"

Charlie and her friends didn't like Lally Richards. She wasn't any fun. She didn't scream and run about and get told off for being noisy, the

way Charlie and her friends did. She never giggled
or told jokes. She just crept around as quiet as a
mouse. *Boring!*

Lally hadn't been asked to Christopher's party.

She hadn't been asked to Charlie's, either.
Charlie and her friends didn't have *anything to do*
with Lally Richards.

"What's she think she's staring at?" said Janine.

Lally blushed, and moved away.

"The nerve!" said Susila.

Charlie put the shoes back in her school bag
and hung the bag on her peg in the cloakroom.

11

Then she went off with the others to class.

Susila was bursting to tell everyone about the silver shoes. She said to Miss Cooper, their class teacher, "Charlie's got some silver ballet shoes!"

Miss Cooper said, "*Silver?* How wonderful! What are they for? Something special?"

"They're for her end-of-year show," said Janine.

"She's going to be a peacock," said Nicole.

After that, people kept coming up to Charlie and begging to be allowed to see the silver shoes.

"At lunchtime," she said.

She felt very important! Almost as if she were a star already.

Except, of course, that she didn't want to be a star. She wanted to be . . . an airline pilot! It was her mom who wanted her to be a star.

At lunchtime she went down to the cloakroom to get her bag. Lots of girls from her class went with her.

"Can we try them on?" begged a girl called Jennifer.

"No!" said Charlie. Jennifer's feet would never fit into Charlie's ballet shoes!

"You'd ruin them." Susila said it sternly. "You can only *look*."

Charlie dipped her hand into her bag. She gave a little squawk of surprise. The shoes weren't there!

"My shoes!" she cried. "They've gone!"

They hunted all over the cloakroom. Under the

benches, under the washbasins, among the coats. No shoes anywhere!

"Where can they be?" wailed Charlie.

Nobody could think. Then Susila suddenly cried, "I saw Lally Richards down here a minute ago!"

"I bet she took them!" said Nicole.

"Find her!" yelled Charlie.

Charlie and her friends went charging off along the corridor. At the end of the corridor there were some stairs that went up and a passage that led to the right.

"I'll go this way!" Charlie pounded off along the passage.

It led to the assembly hall. In the hall was a small stage, where the school put on their own end-of-year shows. Charlie threw open the door—and screeched to a halt. Someone was up there. Someone was dancing. It was Lally!

She was wearing Charlie's new silver shoes . . . .

Charlie stepped forward indignantly. How dare Lally Richards take her shoes! Her precious new shoes!

"What—" began Charlie; and then she stopped. She watched, open-mouthed, as Lally danced back and forth across the stage. Lally was in a world of her own! She had no idea that Charlie was watching her. In her head she was hearing music. And her feet—*in Charlie's new shoes*—were doing what the music told them.

Charlie sucked in her breath. Whoever would have thought it? Little creep-mouse Lally! Floating, drifting, light as a feather! Twisting, turning, glittering like tinsel! Nobody in Charlie's ballet class could dance like that.

All the same, thought Charlie, she shouldn't be wearing my new shoes!

Charlie ran forward, waving her arms.

"Hey!" she cried. "What are you doing?"

Lally stopped dancing. Her pale cheeks turned bright red.

"I'm sorry," she whispered.

"Sorry?" said Charlie. "You jolly well will be sorry if you've gone and messed up my shoes!"

"I haven't! I promise!" Lally slipped her feet out of them and ran toward Charlie, holding the shoes out for inspection. "Look!"

Charlie looked. Grudgingly, she agreed that she couldn't see any marks.

"But they're *my* shoes! You stole them out my bag!"

Lally hung her head. Her lank brown hair fell forward over her shoulders. A moment ago it had been flying out behind her, thick and glossy as a horse's mane.

"What did you do it for?" said Charlie.

A tear trickled its way down Lally's face.

"I just—wanted—to see what it would feel like!"

Charlie frowned. She hadn't meant to make Lally cry!

"What *what* would feel like?" she said.

"Wearing real ballet shoes! I just love to dance," said Lally. "If I had a pair of shoes like this—" she clasped her hands to her chest. Her eyes were shining. "I would dance and dance and never stop!"

"Then they would be full of holes," said Charlie. "It's lucky for you they're not full of holes already. I'm supposed to be wearing these for my end-of-year show!"

The light went out of Lally's eyes. "I shouldn't have taken them."

"No, you shouldn't!"

The two girls stood there, Lally chewing at a fingernail, Charlie holding her shoes.

I *could* report her to Miss Cooper, thought Charlie. Then Lally would get into trouble and serve her right! But she didn't really want to get Lally into trouble. After all, she hadn't done any damage to the shoes, and she *had* said sorry. And she could dance like an angel! Better than anyone Charlie knew.

"I suppose you wouldn't like to do something for me?" said Charlie.

Lally took her finger out of her mouth. "W-what?"

"Take my place at the end-of-year show!"

"T-take your p-place?" Lally's eyes had gone round as soup plates. "But I c-can't dance!"

"You've just *been* dancing," said Charlie.

"I mean—" Lally's finger went back to her mouth. "I've never had lessons."

"Oh! That doesn't matter. I'll teach you. Except that it's got to be our secret," said Charlie. "Just between you and me. Nobody else has got to know! If you'll do it for me," said Charlie recklessly, "I might even let you keep the shoes."

"Won't they be cross?" quavered Lally. "When they discover I'm not you?"

Charlie gave a little chortle.

"They won't know! Not till you're on stage. Then it'll be too late! I know *exactly* how we can do it," said Charlie. "There's this mask, see . . ."

On Saturday, 15th July, two things happened. One was Christopher Carr's party; the other was the Britta Ballet School's end-of-year show. And Charlie Osborne was at both of them!

First of all she was at the end-of-year show. She changed into her costume—her blue dress with the frilly skirt, her peacock mask, her silver shoes—and made her entrance with the corps de ballet. Then, when she came off stage, she scampered along to the cloakroom and quickly gave her costume—and her shoes!—to Lally Richards. Lally was going to dance Charlie's solo.

"Good luck!" whispered Charlie.

Now that the moment had come, Lally was scared. She was trembling!

Charlie squeezed her arm.

"Don't worry," she said. "You'll do it *ever* so much better than I would."

Two minutes later, Lally was on stage, dancing Charlie's solo, while Charlie was whizzing down the road to Christopher's party!

Everyone said how *extraordinary* it was. Charlie was dancing so well today! Better than she had ever danced before!

But Charlie's mom, sitting in the audience, shook her head.

"Whoever that girl is," she said, "she's not my Charlie. She's a superb little dancer . . . but she's not my Charlie!"

Nobody was cross with Lally. Or with Charlie. They were just so excited at the way Lally had danced! Miss Hillary said she was a natural.

Now it's Lally who goes to dancing classes. Charlie's going to be an airline pilot! (Or a policewoman . . . or a deep-sea diver . . .).

Charlie's mom doesn't mind too much. She says she'll be just as proud to have an airline pilot for a daughter. And she's sort of adopted Lally as well. As she says, you can't let talent like that go to waste.

Charlie and Lally have become quite good

friends. Lally came to Charlie's Christmas party and made as much noise as anyone. Nobody thinks she's a creep-mouse any more. Charlie's told them all that some day Lally is going to be a big star.

Oh, and she got to keep the silver shoes! She's worn them so much that they're full of holes . . . .

I DON'T WANT
TO DANCE!

Bel Mooney

Kitty's cousin Melissa had started ballet classes.
"Why don't you go as well, dear?" suggested
Kitty's mom.

"I don't want to dance!" growled Kitty, picking
up her pen to draw a skull and crossbones on her
hand. Mom sighed, looking at Kitty's tousled hair,
dirty nails, and the dungarees all covered in soil—
from where Kitty had been playing Crawling Space
Creatures with William from next door.

"I think it would be nice for you," she said,
"because you'd learn . . . you'd learn . . . Well,
dancing makes you strong."

"No," said Kitty—and that was that.

But when Kitty's big brother Daniel came home
from school and heard about the plan, he laughed.
"Kitty go to ballet!" he screamed. "That's a joke!
She'd dance like a herd of elephants!"

Just then Dad came in, and smiled. "Well, I think she'd dance like Muhammad Ali."

"Who's he?" Kitty asked.

"He was a boxer," grinned Dad.

That did it. If there was one thing Kitty hated it was being teased (although to tell the truth she didn't mind teasing other people!). "Right! I'll show you!" she yelled.

So on Saturday afternoon Kitty was waiting outside the hall with the other girls (and two boys) from the ballet class. Mom had taken her shopping that morning, and Kitty had chosen a black leotard, black tights, and black ballet shoes. Now she saw that all the other girls were in pink. She felt like an ink blot.

Mom went off for coffee with Auntie Susan, leaving Kitty with Melissa and her friend, Emily. They both had their hair done up in a bun, and wore little short net skirts over their leotards. They looked Kitty up and down in a very snooty way.

"You could never be a ballet dancer, Kitty, 'cos you're too clumsy," said Melissa.

"And you're too small," said Emily.

Kitty glared at them. "I don't want to dance anyway," she said. "I'm only coming to this boring old class to please Mom."

But she felt horrid inside, and she wished—oh, how she wished—she was playing in the garden with William. Pirates. Explorers. Cowboys. Crawling Space Creatures. Those were the games they played and Kitty knew they suited her more than ballet class.

She put both hands up to her head and tore out the neat bunches Mom had insisted on. That's better—that's more like *me*, she thought.

Miss Francis, the ballet teacher, was very pretty and graceful, with long black hair in a knot on top of her head. She welcomed Kitty and asked if she had done ballet before.

"No," said Kitty in a small, sulky voice.

"Never mind," said Miss Francis. "You'll soon catch up with the others. Stand in front of me, and watch my feet. Now, class, make rows . . . heels together . . . First position!"

Kitty put her heels together, and tried to put her feet in a straight line, like Miss Francis. But it was very hard. She bent her knees—that made it easier.

There was a giggle from behind.

"Look at Kitty," whispered Emily. "She looks like a duck!"

Miss Francis didn't hear. "Good!" she called. "Now, do you all remember the first position for your arms? Let's see if we can put it all together . . . ." Kitty looked at the girls on each side of her, then at Miss Francis—and put her arms in the air. She stretched up, but was thinking so hard about her arms she forgot what her feet were doing. Then she thought about her feet, and forgot to look up at her arms.

There was an explosion of giggles from behind.

"Kitty looks like a tree in a storm," whispered Melissa.

"Or like a drowning duck!" said Emily.

"Shh, girls!" called Miss Francis with a frown.

And so it went on. Kitty struggled to copy all the positions, but she was always a little bit behind. Once, when Miss Francis went over to speak to the lady playing the piano, she turned around quickly and stuck her tongue out at Melissa and Emily.

Of course, that only made them giggle more. And some of the other children joined in. It wasn't that they wanted to be mean to Kitty—not really. It was just that she looked so funny, with her terrible frown, and her hair sticking out all over the place. And they thought she felt she was better than all of them. But of course the truth was that the horrible feeling inside Kitty was growing so fast she was afraid it would burst out of her eyes.

Everybody seemed so clever and skillful—except her.

"I *am* an ink blot," she thought miserably.

It so happened that Miss Francis was much more than pretty and graceful; she was a very good teacher. She saw Kitty's face and heard the giggles, and knew exactly what was going on. So she clapped her hands and told all the children to sit in a circle.

"Now, we're going to do some free dancing," she said, "so I want some ideas from you all. What could we all be . . .?"

Lots of hands shot up, because the class enjoyed this. "Let's do a flower dance," called Melissa.

"Birds," suggested Emily.

"Let's pretend we're trees . . . and the hurricane comes," called out one of the boys.

"I want to be a flower," Melissa insisted.

Miss Francis looked at Kitty. "What about you? You haven't said anything," she said with a smile.

Kitty shook her head.

"Come on, Kitty, I know you must have an idea. Tell me what we can be when we dance. Just say whatever comes into your head."

"Crawling Space Creatures," said Kitty.

The children began to laugh. But Miss Francis held up her hand. "What a good idea! Tell us a little bit about them first, so we can imagine them . . . ."

"Well, me and William play it in the garden, and

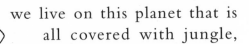

we live on this planet that is all covered with jungle, and we're really horrible-looking things, with no legs, just tentacles like octopuses. And so we move around by crawling, but since we like the food that grows at the top of the bushes we sometimes have to rear up, and that's very hard, see. And we have to be careful, 'cos there's these birds that eat us if they see us, so we have to keep down. Sometimes William is the birds, and tries to get me . . ."

"All right, children—you're all Crawling Space Creatures. We'll see if we can get some spooky, spacelike music on the piano . . . ."

The lady playing the piano smiled and nodded.

So they began. Most of the children loved the idea, but Melissa and Emily and two other girls looked very cross and bored.

"Down on the floor, girls!" called Miss Francis.

Kitty had a wonderful time. She listened to the music, and imagined the strange planet, and twisted her body into all sorts of fantastic shapes. After a few minutes Miss Francis told the others to stop. "All watch Kitty!" she said.

So the children made a circle, and Kitty did her own dance. She lay on the floor and twisted and turned, waving her arms in time to the music. Sometimes she would crouch, then rear up, as if reaching for strange fruit, only to duck down in terror, waving her "tentacles," as the savage birds wheeled overhead . . . .

At last the music stopped, and all the children clapped. Kitty looked up shyly. She had forgotten where she was. She had lost herself in her dance.

When the lesson was over, Miss Francis beckoned Kitty to come over to the piano. None of the children noticed; they were all crowding around the door to meet their mothers.

"Now, Kitty," said Miss Francis quietly, "what do you think you've learned about ballet today?"

"It's hard," said Kitty.

"Well, yes, it is hard. But what else? What about your space dance?"

"That was fun!"

"Because it was *you*?"

Kitty nodded.

"Well, we'll do lots of made-up dances, too, and you'll find you can be lots of things—if you let yourself. That's what modern ballet is all about, you know. Now take this book, and look at the pictures, and you can practice all the positions for next week . . . . You are coming next week?"

Kitty nodded happily, and went off to find Mom. Outside in the hall Melissa and Emily glared at her.

"Look at my tights—they're all dirty," moaned Melissa.

"All that crawling around on the floor—so babyish!" said Emily, in the snootiest voice.

"If you knew anything, you'd know that's what modern ballet is all about," said Kitty, in her most wise and grown-up voice. "I will have to teach you some more about it next week. Now, if you'll just let me by, I'm going to go home and practice."

TEDDY ROBINSON GOES TO THE DANCING CLASS

Joan G. Robinson

One Saturday morning, Teddy Robinson saw that Deborah was putting on her best dress.

"Where are we going?" he said.

"To a dancing class," said Deborah, "to learn to dance. Won't it be fun?"

"What, me?"

"Yes, you can come too. Will you like that?"

"I don't think I'd better dance," said Teddy Robinson, "but I shall like to come and watch."

So he waited while Deborah put on her best socks and shoes, and had a red ribbon tied in her hair; then Deborah brushed his fur with the dolls' hairbrush, and they were all ready to go.

"Oh, my shoes!" said Deborah. "Where are they?"

"On your feet," said Teddy Robinson, surprised.

"No, not these shoes," said Deborah. "I meant my dancing shoes. I've got some new ones. They're very special—pink, with ribbons to keep them on."

"Well I never!" said Teddy Robinson. "You *have* gone grand and grown-up. Fancy having special shoes to dance in!"

Mommy had the new shoes all ready in a bag.

"You can see them when we get there," she said.

So they all set off, Mommy carrying the new shoes, Deborah hopping and skipping all the way, and Teddy Robinson singing to himself as he bounced up and down in her arms:

> *"Hoppity-skippity,*
> *rin-tin-tin—*
> *special shoes for dancing in,*
> *pink, with ribbons—*
> *well, fancy that!*
> *I'd dance myself if I wasn't so fat."*

When they got there Teddy Robinson stopped singing, and Deborah stopped hopping and skipping, and they followed Mommy into the cloakroom. Deborah changed into the new shoes, and had her hair brushed all over again; then they all went into the big hall.

Mary Jane was there, in a pale yellow dress with a frilly petticoat; and Caroline, with pink ribbons to match her party dress; and there was Andrew, in blue corduroy velvet trousers and shoes with silver buckles on them.

"Hello, Teddy Robinson," said Andrew. "Have you come to dance?"

"Not today," said Teddy Robinson. "I didn't bring my shoes."

"He is going to watch," said Deborah, and she put him down on an empty chair in the front row. Then she ran off to talk to Mary Jane and Caroline.

All the mothers and aunties and nannies who had come to watch the class were chatting together in the rows of chairs behind Teddy Robinson, and on the chair next to him sat a large walkie-talkie doll, wearing a pink frilled dress with a ribbon sash. She was sitting up very straight, smiling and staring in front of her.

Teddy Robinson wondered whether to speak to her, but just then a lady came in and sat down at the piano, and a moment later the teacher, whose name was Miss Silver, came into the hall.

Teddy Robinson decided he had better not start talking now, as the class was about to begin. Instead he listened to all the mothers and aunties and nannies, who had all begun talking to the children at once, in busy, whispering voices.

"Stand up nicely, point your toes."

"Here's your hankie, blow your nose."

"Don't be shy now, do your best. Make it up and follow the rest."

"Where's your hankie? Did you blow?"

"There's the music. Off you go!"

Then the children all ran into the middle of the floor, and the dancing class began.

Teddy Robinson, sitting tidily on his chair in the front row, thought how jolly it was to be one of the grown-ups who had come to watch, and how lucky he was to belong to the nicest little girl in the class.

"How pretty she looks in her new pink shoes and her red ribbon," he said to himself. "And how well she can dance already! She is doing it quite differently from all the others. When they are doing *hop, one-two-three* she is doing *one-two-three, hop, hop, hop*, and it looks so much jollier that way. She is the only one able to do it right. None of the others can keep up with her."

He smiled proudly as Deborah went dancing past, her eyes shining, her red ribbon flying.

A lady in the row behind whispered to someone else, "Who is that little girl with the red ribbon, the one who hops three times instead of once?"

The other lady whispered back, "I don't know. She is new, you can see that—but isn't she enjoying herself? That's her teddy bear on the chair in front."

Teddy Robinson pretended he wasn't listening and hummed softly to himself in time to the music. He was pleased that other people had noticed Deborah too. He looked sideways at the walkie-talkie doll. She was still smiling, and watching the dancing carefully. Teddy Robinson was glad to think that she, too, was admiring Deborah.

When the music stopped and the children paused for breath Teddy Robinson turned to her.

"Aren't you dancing?" he asked.

"No," said the doll; "I walk and talk, but I don't dance. I've come to watch."

"I've come to watch too," said Teddy Robinson.

"I suppose you don't dance either?" said the doll, looking at Teddy Robinson's fat tummy.

"No, I sing," said Teddy Robinson.

"Ah, yes," said the doll, "you have the figure for it."

The children began dancing again, and the lady at the piano played such hoppity-skippity music that Teddy Robinson couldn't help joining in with a little song, very quietly to himself:

> *"Hoppity-skippity, one-two-three,*
> *The bestest dancer belongs to me.*
> *Oh, what a fortunate bear I be!*
> *Hoppity-skippity, one-two-three."*

The walkie-talkie doll turned to Teddy Robinson.

"How beautifully she dances!" she said. "I'm not surprised so many people have come to watch her."

"Thank you," said Teddy Robinson, bowing slightly, and feeling very proud. "Yes, she does dance well and this is her first lesson."

"Oh, no, it's not," said the doll. "I bring her every Saturday. She's had quite a number of lessons already."

"I beg your pardon," said Teddy Robinson. "Who are we talking about?"

"My little girl, Mary, of course," said the doll, "the one with the yellow curls."

"Oh," said Teddy Robinson, "I thought we were talking about my little girl, Deborah, the one with the red ribbon."

The doll didn't seem to hear. She was staring at the children with a fixed smile. Miss Silver was arranging them in two rows, the girls on one side, the boys on the other.

Teddy Robinson and the walkie-talkie doll both kept their eyes fixed on the girls' row.

"She looks so pretty, doesn't she?" said the doll. "I do admire her dress, don't you?"

"Yes," said Teddy Robinson, looking at Deborah.

"That pale blue suits her so well," said the doll.

"Thank you," said Teddy Robinson, "I'm glad you like it; but it isn't pale blue—it's white."

"Oh, no, it's pale blue," said the doll. "I helped her mother to choose it myself."

Teddy Robinson looked puzzled.

"Are you talking about the little girl with the red hair ribbon?" he asked.

"No, of course not," said the doll. "Why should I be? I'm talking about Mary."

"Whoever is Mary?" said Teddy Robinson.

"The little girl we have all come to watch," said the doll. "*My* little girl. We've been talking about her all the time."

"*I* haven't," said Teddy Robinson. "I've been talking about Deborah."

"Deborah?" said the doll. "Whoever is Deborah?"

"What a silly creature this doll is!" said Teddy Robinson to himself. "She doesn't seem able to keep her mind on the class at all." And he decided not to bother about talking to her any more. Instead he listened to Miss Silver, who was teaching the boys and girls how to bow and curtsy to each other.

"I must watch this carefully," said Teddy Robinson to himself. "I should like to know how to bow properly—it might come in handy at any time. I might be asked to tea at Buckingham Palace or happen to meet the Queen out shopping one day, and I should look very silly if I didn't know how to make my bow properly."

As the boys all bowed from the waist Teddy Robinson leaned forward on his chair.

"Lower!" cried Miss Silver.

The boys all bowed lower, and Teddy Robinson

leaned forward as far as he could; but he went just a little too far, and a moment later he fell head over heels onto the floor. Luckily, no one knew he had been practicing his bow, they just thought he had toppled off his chair by mistake, as anyone might— so they took no notice of him.

Then it was the girls' turn to curtsy. The line of little girls wobbled and wavered, and Deborah wobbled so much that she, too, fell on the floor. But after three tries she did manage to curtsy without falling over, and Teddy Robinson was very proud of her.

"Nevermind," said Miss Silver, as she said goodbye to them at the end of the class. "You did very well for a first time. You can't expect to learn to dance in one lesson. But you did enjoy it, didn't you?"

"Oh, yes!" said Deborah. "It was lovely."

"What did she mean?" said Teddy Robinson, as soon as they were outside. "I thought you danced better than anybody."

"Oh, no," said Deborah. "I think I was doing it all wrong, but it *was* fun. I'm glad we're going again next Saturday."

"Well I never!" said Teddy Robinson. "I quite thought you were the only one doing it right. Never mind. Did you see when I fell off the chair? That was me trying to bow. I don't think I did it very well either."

"You did very well for a first time, too," said Deborah. "You can't expect to learn to bow in one lesson. We must practice together at home, though. You can learn to bow to me while I practice doing my curtsy."

"That will be very nice," said Teddy Robinson. "Then next time we shan't both end up on the floor."

That night Teddy Robinson had a most Beautiful Dream. He dreamt he was in a very large theater, with red velvet curtains, tied with large golden tassels, on each side of the stage.

Every seat in the theater was full; Teddy
Robinson himself was sitting in the middle of the
front row, and all the people were watching
Deborah, who was dancing all alone on the stage
in her new pink dancing shoes. She was dressed
like a princess, in a frilly white dress with a red
sash, and she had a silver crown on her head.

The orchestra was playing sweetly, and Deborah was dancing so beautifully that soon everyone was whispering and asking who she was.

Teddy Robinson heard someone behind him saying, "She belongs to that handsome bear in the front row, the one in the velvet suit and lace collar."

Teddy Robinson looked around, but couldn't see any bear in a velvet suit and lace collar. Then he looked down and saw that instead of his ordinary trousers he was wearing a suit of beautiful blue velvet, with a large lace collar fastened at the neck with a silver pin. And in his lap was a bunch of roses tied with silver ribbon.

"Goodness gracious, they must have meant me!" he thought, and felt his fur tingling with pleasure and excitement.

As the music finished and Deborah came to the front of the stage to curtsy, Teddy Robinson felt himself floating through the air with his bunch of roses, and a moment later he landed lightly on the stage beside her. A murmur went up from the audience, "Ah, here is Teddy Robinson himself!"

Folding one paw neatly across his tummy, he bowed low to Deborah. Then, as she took the roses from him and they both bowed and curtsied again, everyone in the theater clapped so loudly that Teddy Robinson woke up and found he was in bed beside Deborah.

At first he was so surprised that he could hardly

believe he was really at home in bed, but just then Deborah woke up, too. She rolled over, smiling, with her eyes shut, and said, "Oh, Teddy Robinson, I've just had such a Beautiful Dream! I must tell you all about it."

So she did. And the funny thing was that Deborah had dreamt exactly the same dream as Teddy Robinson. She remembered every bit of it.

And that is the end of the story about how Teddy Robinson went to the dancing class.

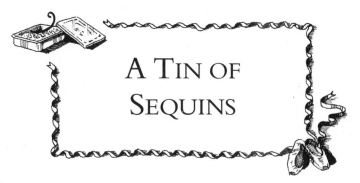

A Tin of
Sequins

Caroline Plaisted

"My Aunty Joyce is a ballet wardrobe mistress," Caroline used to tell her friends in the playground at school. "She makes tutus for all the ballerinas so that they can twirl around on the stage like fairies."

Caroline loved going to visit her aunt at work. Aunty Joyce worked at the Opera House—the same Opera House where Caroline's mom had danced when she was a ballerina.

Caroline thought the ballet wardrobe was a brilliant place. It wasn't anything like the wardrobe she had at home in her bedroom. Instead it was a great big room crammed with magical things. There were rails of ballet costumes all along the walls. Tutus of every color hung next to floaty dresses like the ones that the queens in fairy tales wear. Rats' costumes from *The Nutcracker* and

Squirrel Nutkin from *The Tales of Beatrix Potter* were on another rail, alongside brightly colored unitards from contemporary ballets. There were even the glittering jackets that the Prince in *The Sleeping Beauty* wore, which sparkled under the worklamps around the room.

On one side of the wardrobe there were shelves neatly stacked with buff-colored boxes. Aunty Joyce had once shown Caroline the treasure that each box held: wigs, masks, ornate headdresses, gloves, and props like walking sticks and magic wands. Each box was labeled with the name of the ballet and the character who wore what was kept inside it: the wigs of the Ugly Sisters in *Cinderella*;

Jeremy Fisher's webbed feet; even Juliet's mask from the ball in *Romeo and Juliet*.

As always, when Caroline arrived at the ballet wardrobe, Aunty Joyce gave her a squeezy hug.

"Hello, my special girl. My goodness, am I pleased to see you—I need you to do an important job for me. Will you go around with my pin magnet and collect all the pins and needles that I've dropped since you last came?"

Aunty Joyce sat down on a stool next to a gigantic wooden table and handed Caroline her magnet. It was as big as both her hands. As Aunty Joyce and Caroline's mom sat down to a cup of coffee and a chat, Caroline set to work at once. She crawled around the table legs, taking care not to put her knees on any of the pins. Then she scrambled out from underneath and looked around, wondering where to go next with the magnet.

Over by the windows there was a row of sewing machines where people were busy sewing bodices onto the skirts of tutus and stitching on the arms of unitards. Caroline was sure that this would be a place worth a visit with the magnet.

"Excuse me," she said as she quickly sucked up the pins and other shiny metal things that were scattered all around the seamstresses' feet. Some of the needles still had sewing thread hanging from them and the pins, which stuck quickly to the magnet, got caught up in the cotton and fluff. Next, Caroline moved over to the rails of costumes to see what she could find on the floor there. When she had finished, the magnet was a mass of silvery treasures which she presented to Aunty Joyce.

"My goodness—what a great collection, Caroline! Now, you pull up that stool and let's see what we've got."

Between them, Aunty Joyce and Caroline sorted the bits and pieces that were on the magnet. Pins went in one pile, needles in another, and the straggly bits of sewing thread and fluff went straight in the bin. But there was one more pile—the best pile of all. This was full of silver sequins, fluorescent blue teardrop shaped beads, golden crescent moon shapes that looked as if they were made of real

gold, and transparent beads—
some of them tinted with the
palest of colors. Aunty Joyce
held them up to the light and
told Caroline which costume
each one had come from.

First was a glass bead that shone
like crystal as it caught the reflection
of the light. "We used ones like this on the Black
Queen's costume in *Swan Lake*. And these frosted
sequins hung just like icicles from the ballerina in
The Snow Queen."

Aunty Joyce handed each one to Caroline as she
spoke about them and Caroline cupped them in
her hands as if they were precious gems. She could
imagine just how special she'd feel in one of Aunty
Joyce's costumes, shimmering with jewels. In her
head, Caroline was twirling around on the stage of
the Opera House, her tutu twinkling and sparkling
under the lights.

Caroline smiled and continued to finger the
beads and sequins. They felt cool and smooth in
her hand as she dreamt of starring in *The Sleeping
Beauty*. But instead of a handsome prince waking
her from her slumber, it was Aunty Joyce.

"I don't think I need those ones any more. Why
don't I put them in this," she opened the drawer
under the huge wooden table and pulled out a
little blue tin—"and then you could take them

home with you. Perhaps you could sew them onto your doll's tutu so that she looks like one of the ballerinas here at the Opera House."

"Oh, thanks, Aunty Joyce," Caroline said, taking the tin and placing her new treasures carefully inside it. And when she left at the end of the afternoon, she promised to come back soon to help Aunty Joyce collect up the pins and sequins again.

That night in bed Caroline clutched the little blue tin to her chest. She thought about sewing some of the sequins onto her doll's tutu as Aunty Joyce had suggested. But then she changed her mind. She knew exactly what she was going to do with them—she was going to keep them in the tin. Then every time she went to see Aunty Joyce she could take the tin with her and put in it any more treasures she might find in the ballet wardrobe. And one day, when she was a ballerina herself, perhaps Aunty Joyce would make her a special tutu that she'd sew the collection of sequins onto.

In fact, Caroline didn't have to wait too long before Aunty Joyce made a costume for her. She was chosen to be one of the rats in *The Nutcracker* that Christmas. It was great to be in the ballet— Caroline was the rat that jumped out of the darkness on the tenth chime of midnight. Her rat costume didn't have any sequins or beads on it, and it looked a bit straggly and limp as it dangled from the hanger on the costume rail in the wardrobe.

48

But when Caroline stepped into the costume and pulled up the tights, which had padding on the thighs, and then put her arms into the sleeves, which had gloves attached, complete with claws, her transformation into a rat began. The final touch was the rat's mask. When she put it on, she could see through the holes that were cut out of the mask, but all the audience could see was a pair of little black, beady eyes shining under the stagelights. On the rat's muzzle were thick black whiskers which looked a bit like liquorice.

In the New Year, *The Nutcracker* came to the end of its season and Caroline had to put her rat costume back on the rail for the last time. It didn't sparkle and shimmer like a ballerina's tutu, but she had loved wearing it just as much and was sad to say goodbye to the rat that had given her a chance to appear on stage. On her last afternoon at the Opera House, Aunty Joyce came along to see her in the dressing room that she shared with the other rats.

"I know you haven't got time to help me with the

49

magnet today, Caroline, but I've brought something along that's a bit different for you to add to that tin of yours."

Caroline held out her hand and Aunty Joyce popped a little black coil into it. Caroline looked down and circled her finger around the smooth object. It was a whisker. A rat's whisker—just like the ones on her costume. Aunty Joyce had saved it especially for her.

Caroline knew that sequins and beads were beautiful. But then so was a rat's whisker, if someone had made it just for you.

ROSIE, THE LITTLE BALLERINA

Gelsey Kirkland and Greg Lawrence

M iss Bradley had taped up a sign on the glass of the front door, and it said:

THIS IS STRICTLY A BALLET STUDIO.
I DO NOT OFFER TAP, JAZZ, OR
BALLROOM DANCING.
BEGINNER AND INTERMEDIATE
CLASSES AVAILABLE.

PLEASE TAKE OFF YOUR SHOES.

Miss Bradley made up this rule that you couldn't wear your shoes in the studio. You had to take them off at the front door, like people do over in Japan, and then you put on a pair of these fluffy pink or blue slippers that Miss Bradley kept in a rack out by the door. Some of the parents who came into the studio really didn't like having to take their shoes off at all. Like my dad. He always just waited around for me outside whenever he came to pick me up from class.

Anyway, this afternoon I took off my sneakers and put on my own pair of black ballet slippers. Then I hurried down the hall. When I got to the dressing room, I was so nervous I could feel my heart pounding in my chest. I rushed right inside because I had only about two minutes to change. Miss Bradley didn't make us wear uniforms like some other teachers do. She just said that since we were each different on the inside, there was no need for us to look the same on the outside. Miss Bradley did say that we should always be neat and not try to hide our bodies with clothes that were too baggy. Up until Miss Bradley came to Riverview two years ago, I used to take class from Mrs. Grant. She made us all wear pink tights and pink leotards. But then Mrs. Grant moved out of town somewhere, and Miss Bradley took over running the studio and changed the rules.

Another one of her rules was that if you were late, then you weren't allowed to take class that day. So I was in really big trouble if I got there late for my first pointe class. That was what my heart was telling me and why my stomach was sort of doing flip-flops. I was the last person to get to the dressing room, and just as I was going in, Cynthia Anderson and Deidre Larson passed me in the doorway on their way out. Cynthia stopped long enough to say, "Ya better hurry up. The teacher's little pet can't be late now, can she? We'll tell Miss Bradley you're on your way, Rosie."

"Don't do me any favors, Cynthia," I said. I guess I sounded a little nasty, but Cynthia was going on and on lately how I was the teacher's pet, and that really burned me up. She called me that just because I worked harder at dancing than she did, and once in a while Miss Bradley asked me to demonstrate a step for the rest of the class. Even when we were younger, Cynthia always used to call me names. Like Carrot-Head and Twinkle-Toes. For some reason that really got me mad, and we almost got into a fight in the schoolyard when we were in Fourth Grade. My mom once told me to remember sticks and stones could break my bones, but words could never hurt me. But I didn't believe that for a second. Those names Cynthia called me hurt a lot sometimes.

Of course, she never said anything in front of grown-ups, so I knew I'd be safe once I went in the studio. Then Cynthia would probably be too busy checking herself in the mirror to say anything else to me anyway. Only today, it turned out, there was no mirror! Miss Bradley had put curtains up over all the mirrors in the studio. I found that out when I rushed in and almost ran into Miss Bradley, who was just closing the door. She told me, "Slow down, Rosie. I hope you remembered to sign in outside."

"Oh, Miss Bradley, I forgot!" I said. "I didn't want to be late and miss class."

"Don't worry about it now," she told me. "Just make sure you sign in before you leave."

It was one o'clock on the dot. After I left the saddlebag with my pointe shoes at the side of the studio, I put some rosin on my slippers to keep them from slipping and sliding over the wood floor. There was a box of rosin in the corner that you scuffed and stamped your shoes in so the bottoms would be covered with rosin dust. One time I got dust in my eyes and practically had to leave class because I couldn't stop the tears from coming out of my eyes. So I was careful not to get any rosin on my hands. I found a place at one of the portable *barres* near the back of the room and got ready for the first exercise.

That was when I saw this big smirk on Cynthia's face. She was right next to me, but I just ignored

her. Emily was on the other side of me. There were only ten girls taking class. Miss Bradley stood near the center of the floor and told us, "I'm doing us all a big favor today by not letting you watch yourselves. You may remember me telling you that ballet is a very special way we use our bodies to tell a story. That story must always come from our hearts, and that's why we practice all of these steps and positions in every class. Believe me, ladies, you'll never become ballerinas by staring in the mirror. You have to learn to see beyond that mirror so the audience can see with you."

I didn't know exactly what Miss Bradley meant, but I was pretty glad not to have to look at myself in the mirror because a lot of times I couldn't help comparing my body to the other girls like Cynthia and Deidre and Jennifer Taylor, and I really didn't feel too hot when I did that. Sometimes I wanted to hide. I mean, I'm short, and I have these really, really long arms that go almost all the way to my knees. No kidding. My mom says that being pretty is just all in your head, but my head tells me I'm just never going to be pretty like those other girls.

I tried not to get down in the dumps about it, and I felt better once we started doing exercises at the *barre*. The music always made me happy. It was fun the way you had to try to keep ahead of the beat. The pianist, Mrs. Quill, always played for Miss Bradley's classes. She had long, shiny silver hair, and the fingers of her hands were real long. They looked like they were made out of ivory or something, just like the keys of the piano that she was playing.

Sometimes Miss Bradley got so excited that she just sang out loud over the music, and then she'd scream at us to tell us what we were doing wrong. No matter how well we did a step, it seemed like it was almost never good enough. But then it was fun when you finally got it right, or almost right. My favorite part of the class was right after the *barre*, when we did jumps across the floor. I was sure that I was the best jumper in the class. Even though I'm so short, I could still go higher in the air and farther across the floor than anybody else when I did a *grand jeté*.

If you don't know anything about ballet, then you might not know all of the steps have French names. Like *plié*, and *tendu*, and *grande battement*. I used to think the names sounded funny. But after Miss Bradley taught us what they meant and how we were supposed to do each of the steps, they didn't sound funny to me any more. We always started at the *barre* with *pliés*, which was where you sort of bent your knees and went down and up. But when you were going down, you were supposed to think of going up. And when you were going up, you were supposed to think that you were going down. Boy, was that ever confusing for

me at first. One time Miss Bradley told me, "Try to resist the direction in which your body is moving, Rosie, and keep turning out your heart to the audience."

I liked that stuff about the heart and making believe that I was on a stage in front of an audience. But by the end of the *barre* exercises it was hard to make believe anything because I was so pooped. Miss Bradley told us it was time to put on our pointe shoes and try going up on our toes. I went over and grabbed my saddlebag and took out my shoes and ribbons. After I got them on and all, I saw Cynthia pointing down at my legs. She turned to Miss Bradley, and then said with this loud voice that sounded so phoney, "Miss Bradley, are we supposed to tie our ribbons way up around our knees the way Rosie has them?" I looked down and saw that my ribbons came to the tops of my calves, where I had tied them in a bow. Cynthia laughed, and then she said, "Rosie looks like she has bowed legs and bows on her knees."

I started blushing, but Miss Bradley said to me in her soft voice, "You might lower those ribbons just a bit, Rosie, and tie them more neatly."

She showed me where to tie them above my ankles, and then we all took our places again at the *barre*. I looked at Cynthia, and she was smirking again. But now I was more worried about my toe shoes fitting so tight. Boy, they really hurt my feet even when I just walked slowly in them. I looked around at the other girls to see if their shoes hurt them too, like my mom said. But their faces were really just kind of blank and tense, and everybody looked awfully serious. I was holding my breath and squeezing the *barre* with both hands.

Miss Bradley said, "Now, I know your little feet must hurt in those brand-new shoes, but you'll break them in and get over that soon enough." None of us even dared say a word. It was really quiet. Then Miss Bradley cried out, "You all look like you're constipated. Relax and try breathing. Honestly, ladies. Those feet are not going to fall off. I promise you." After she said that, she screwed up her face and imitated the way we looked. Then it was like all of a sudden all of us just let out our breath and groaned and laughed at the same time.

I felt better after that. Miss Bradley said, "Now we're going to roll up on pointe, and roll back down through the feet to the floor. I want you to start with your feet parallel in sixth position. Both hands close together on the *barre*. We're going to repeat this eight times. Don't forget those upper bodies of yours."

Miss Bradley asked Mrs. Quill to play something at a slow tempo, an adagio. Then all of us tried to go up on pointe, but it was an awful lot harder than it looked. I felt like an elephant was stepping on my toes. Miss Bradley told us not to hike up our shoulders and not to drop our chests, but how

was I ever supposed to remember exactly what to do with every part of my body at the same time? Every time I fixed one part of me, some other part would go wrong. And my knees kept wanting to buckle under me every time I tried to go up on my toes.

Miss Bradley came around behind me and said, "Don't worry, Rosie. When your feet become more flexible, you'll be able to keep your knees straighter." Miss Bradley's eyes always seemed to sparkle when she talked. But what she said next made my heart go right into my throat. "I want everyone to watch Rosie show us how we roll down through the foot and reach all the way up to heaven at the same time. The rest of you are dropping onto your heels. Now, make a circle around Rosie."

All of a sudden everybody was looking at me, and I wished that I could turn invisible. Miss Bradley was standing a few feet in front of me on the other side of the portable *barre*. She told me, "This time, Rosie, before you go up on your toes, I want you to think of someone you really love, and imagine them standing right here where I am. Okay? Just make believe for a minute you're Juliet reaching out for your Romeo. I want you to tell him how you feel with your heart. Say, "I love you, Romeo."

I did what Miss Bradley said, but I thought of

my horse, Sugar, when I had to think of someone that I really loved. It took for ever to get up on my toes, but reaching for Sugar somehow made it seem easier. I kept reaching for him even when I was going back down to the floor. When I was finished, I didn't know if I had done it right or not. But all of a sudden Miss Bradley yelled out, "Brava! That was beautiful, Rosie."

When she said that, my throat felt tight. I was so happy, I was afraid I might cry. I really had to look away when some of the other girls clapped. I was sort of happy and embarrassed at the same time. Afterwards, in the dressing room, I got dressed as fast as I could and got my things together to leave. Emily asked me why I was in such a hurry, and I just told her I was late. Cynthia glared at me as I was going out of the door with my saddlebag tucked under my arm. Just before I heard the door close, I heard her say to the other girls still inside, "There goes the teacher's pet." But I didn't care at all. I could hardly wait to get back and tell Sugar what had happened in class.

He was waiting for me in front of the barbershop. And so was Uncle Max. I thanked Uncle Max for watching Sugar for me, and then Sugar and I started for home. While I was leading him down Main Street, Miss Bradley drove past us in her car and looked out of the window at me for a second. She had kind of a funny expression on

her face. But I waved to her and told Sugar, "That's Miss Bradley, my ballet teacher."

I was happy all day, even though I did keep wondering to myself about that weird look Miss Bradley had given me. Later that night, after I'd told my mom at the dinner table all about class, I went straight up to my room, and jumped up and down on my bed for a while. I guess I do get pretty excited sometimes. But I knew that Sugar would know just how I felt, and I wrote him a letter in my diary.

Dear Sugar,

It's a little hard explaining
what I learned in class today,
You see, my ballet teacher taught me
how to speak in a silent way.
She answered all these questions
that were inside me all along;
Now I no longer have the feeling
that I'm doing something wrong.
Sugar, there's certainly no reason
you'd be interested in ballet,
Except that when we jump a fence,
you've done a grand jeté*!*

Of course, one thing that's different
     between your big jump and mine
Is that only if I stretch both knees
     will Miss Bradley say, "It's fine."
She can be very strict, and very stern,
     so it's her I strive to impress,
But today was special because she said
     it's love we must try to express.
Oh, Sugar, I can't wait till morning,
     when I come to clean your stall,
Then I can show you in my toe shoes
     how love can grow so tall!

OUT OF STEP

Jean Richardson

"I'm going to be a ballet dancer when I grow up," said Rachel firmly.

Her sister Rebecca—who liked to be called Becky—looked surprised. She was usually the one who had the ideas.

Because they were identical twins, everyone expected them to be alike—but they weren't. While Rachel was as graceful as a swan, Becky was as clumsy as a baby elephant.

"Perhaps dancing classes will be fun," Becky said doubtfully, "but I think I'd rather be an actress. I'm much better at talking."

But Mom agreed with Rachel, and when they went to buy some dance clothes, Becky enjoyed the shop crammed with all kinds of dance costumes. She darted around, tugging dresses off the racks, and fell in love with the stiff little skirts called tutus. When she looked in the mirror, she saw herself floating across the stage on tiptoe.

"You won't be needing skirts like that yet," said the assistant. "Beginners need leotards and cardigans and long socks to keep their muscles warm."

"Can I have an orange and purple leotard?" asked Becky, who liked to be different.

"The school says pink or blue with white cardigans," Mom said, hoping Becky wouldn't be difficult.

"Looks nicer with the slippers," added the assistant.

Neither twin could wait to try on the pink satin ballet shoes.

By the end of the first term, Becky knew she'd never be a dancer.

Rachel's feet did as they were told. Becky's had a mind of their own. Rachel's arms made pretty, curving lines. Becky's drooped like flowers gasping for water.

Rachel danced in time to the music. Becky listened to what the music was

saying—and forgot all about keeping time. As their teacher, Mrs. Fishwick, said, not meaning to be unkind, "You'd never think they were twins."

One day, Mrs. Fishwick had some exciting news for the class.

"The famous ballerina Natalie Seymour is coming to our end-of-term show. She started her training at this school—I remember when she was your age—and we shall have to be on our toes to impress her. Our performance has got to be perfect."

"Can I do . . . Can I wear . . . Can we . . ." Everyone was suddenly talking at once—everyone except Becky. For once, she had nothing to say.

"There's no way I can impress a ballerina," she thought miserably. "If only I could dance like Rachel."

From then on the class spent all their time rehearsing. Rachel was the wind that danced through the flowers. Becky was one of the flowers.

"I wish I could do something else," said Becky crossly, after Mrs. Fishwick had again caught her turning right when all the other flowers turned left. "Why can't I tell the audience what's happening?"

"We let our feet tell the story," said Mrs. Fishwick, moving Becky into the back row with the boys, who were supposed to be trees.

Rachel felt very sorry for her twin. Becky did try to be graceful, but she waved her arms so eagerly that she nearly hit Rachel in the eye.

As the star of the show, Rachel was to present a bouquet to Natalie Seymour. She was thrilled— until Mrs. Fishwick told her she'd have to make a speech.

"I know I'll get it wrong," she wailed to Becky. "I'm good at dancing, not speaking. I'm good at remembering steps, not words. Can you hear me say it again?"

But not this time, next time, nor the time after could she get the words right.

"I wish I could do it," said Becky, who by now knew Rachel's speech off by heart. "I'd much rather make a speech than do that silly dance."

Then the twins looked at each other and had the same idea . . . .

On the great day, Rachel helped Becky pin up her hair and made sure that for once the ribbons of her shoes weren't twisted. When they were ready and looked in the mirror, it was impossible to tell them apart.

"Let's practice the curtsy again," suggested Rachel.

Becky tried to sink down and rise up gracefully, but somehow her feet got tangled up.

"No, like this," said Rachel, but she was laughing so much that she ended up on the floor as well.

There were so many important people waiting to greet Natalie Seymour that even Becky was a little scared. She felt a shiver of excitement as a large, shiny car drove up and the photographers hoisted their cameras.

Flashlights flickered on all sides as the ballerina stepped out of the car and smiled. Becky felt very small, but very important, too.

Now it was her turn to play the star part.

Becky made her speech so beautifully that no one noticed that she didn't curtsy. She was enjoying herself so much that she couldn't resist chattering on to Natalie Seymour.

"My sister's going to be a famous dancer like you," she told her, "but I'm hopeless at dancing. Mrs. Fishwick says I've got two left feet."

Natalie Seymour smiled. "Perhaps you're better at talking than dancing," she said.

By now Mrs. Fishwick had guessed that the chatterbox wasn't Rachel—and it gave her an idea. "Becky dear, why don't you stay with our guest and tell her about our ballet. You're just the right person to explain it."

Rachel, who was waiting in the wings, had no

idea what was going on. She'd expected to find Becky with the rest of the class, but when she stole a look at the audience, there she was in the front row, sitting next to Natalie Seymour.

Rachel suddenly realized that for once she was on her own. Becky was thinking how glad she was not to be dancing when she sensed that Rachel needed her. The twins had always been able to read each other's thoughts, especially if they were in trouble. It was as though she could hear Rachel saying, "I want to dance so much, but I'm scared. I can't do it in front of all those people."

Becky shut her eyes, crossed her fingers, and willed Rachel to dance. "It's only stage fright," she told her. "You'll be fine once you start."

But not until she heard the audience clap and someone shout "Brava," did Becky dare to open her eyes.

"What a talented pair you are," said Natalie Seymour, when Becky dragged a shy but triumphant Rachel to meet her. "Becky tells me you want to be a dancer. If you're prepared to work very hard, perhaps one day you will be. And I'm sure I haven't heard the last of Becky. On the stage or on television, perhaps?"

The twins were very proud of each other. Rachel grabbed Becky and whirled her into a dance of joy—and for once both of them knew just the right steps.

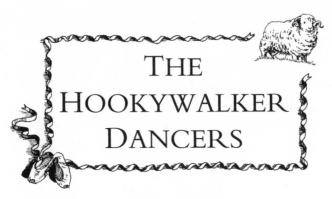

THE HOOKYWALKER DANCERS

Margaret Mahy

In the heart of the great city of Hookywalker was the School of Dramatic Art. It was full of all sorts of actors and singers and wonderful clowns, but the most famous of them all was the great dancer, Brighton.

Brighton could leap like an antelope and spin like a top. He was as slender as a needle. In fact, when he danced you almost expected little stitches to follow him across the stage. Every day he did his exercises at the *barre* to music played on his tape recorder.

"One and a *plié* and a stretch, two-three, and *port de bras* and back to first!" he counted. He exercised so gracefully that, outside the School of Dramatic Art, pedlars rented ladders so that lovers of the dance could climb up and look through the window at Brighton practicing.

Of course, life being what it is, many other dancers were often jealous of him. I'm afraid that most of them ate too much and were rather fat, whereas Brighton had an elegant figure. They pulled his chair away from under him when he sat down, or tried to trip him up in the middle of his dancing, but Brighton was so graceful he simply made falling down look like an exciting new part of the dance, and the people standing on ladders clapped and cheered and banged happily on the windows.

Although he was such a graceful dancer, Brighton was not conceited. He led a simple life. For instance, he didn't own a car, travelling everywhere on roller-skates, his tape recorder clasped to his ear. Not only this, he did voluntary work

for the Society for Bringing Happiness to Dumb Beasts. At the weekends he would put on special performances for pets and farm animals. Savage dogs became quiet as lambs after watching Brighton dance, and nervous sheep grew wool thicker than ever before. Farmers from outlying districts would ring up the School of Dramatic Art and ask if they could hire Brighton to dance to their cows, and many a parrot, temporarily off its seed, was brought back to full appetite by seeing Brighton dance the famous solo called *The Noble Savage in the Lonely Wood*.

Brighton had a way of kicking his legs up that suggested deep sorrow, and his *demi-pliés* regularly brought tears to the eyes of the parrots, after which they tucked into their seed quite ravenously.

One day, the director of the School of Dramatic Art called Brighton to his office.

"Brighton," he said, "I have an urgent request here from a farmer who needs help with a flock of very nervous sheep. He is in despair!"

"Glad to help!" said Brighton in his graceful fashion. "What seems to be the trouble?"

"Wolves—that's what the trouble is!" cried the director. "He lives on the other side of the big forest, and a pack of twenty wolves comes out of the forest early every evening and tries to devour some of his prize merinos. It's disturbing the sheep very badly. They get nervous twitches, and their wool is falling out from shock."

"I'll set off at once," Brighton offered. "I can see it's an urgent case."

"It's a long way," the director said, doubtfully. "It's right on the other side of the forest."

"That's all right," said Brighton. "I have my trusty roller-skates, and the road is tarred all the way. I'll take my tape recorder to keep me company, and I'll get there in next to no time."

"That's very fast," the director said in a respectful voice. "Oh, Brighton, I wish all my dancers were like you! Times are hard for the School of Dramatic Art. A lot of people are staying at home and watching car crashes on television. They don't want art—they want danger, they want battle, murder, and sudden death—and it's becoming much harder to run the school at a profit. If all our dancers were as graceful as you there would be no problem at all, but as you know a lot of them are just a whisker on the fat side. They don't do their exercises the way they should."

Little did he realize that the other dancers were actually listening at the keyhole, and when they heard this critical remark they all began to sizzle with jealousy. You could hear them sizzling with it.

"I'll show him who's fat and who isn't," muttered a very spiteful dancer called Antoine. "Where are Brighton's skates?"

Brighton's skates were, in fact, in the cloakroom under the peg on which he hung his beret and his great billowing cape. It was but the work of a moment to loosen one or two vital grommets. The skates looked all right, but they were no longer as safe as skates ought to be.

"There," said Antoine, laughing nastily. "They'll hold together for a little bit, but once he gets into the forest they'll collapse, and we'll see how he gets on then, all alone with the wind and the wolves—and without wheels."

The halls of the School of Dramatic Art rang with the jealous laughter of the other dancers as they slunk off in all directions. A minute later Brighton came in, suspecting nothing, put on his beret and his great billowing cape, strapped on his skates, and set off, holding his tape recorder to his ear.

Now, during the day, the wolves spent a long time snoozing and licking their paws clean in a clearing on top of the hill. From there they had a good view of the Hookywalker road. They could look out in all directions and even see as far as Hookywalker when the air was clear. It happened that their present king was a great thinker, and something was worrying him deeply.

"I know we're unpopular," sighed the King of the Wolves, "but what can I do about it? It's the nature of things that wolves steal a few sheep here and there. It's part of the great pattern of nature." Though this seemed reasonable he was frowning and brooding as he spoke. "Sometimes—I don't know—I feel there must be more to life than just ravening around, grabbing the odd sheep, and howling at the moon."

"Look!" cried the wolf who was on look-out duty. "Someone is coming down the great road from the city."

"How fast he's going!" said another wolf. "And whatever is it he is holding to his ear?"

"Perhaps he has an earache," suggested a female wolf in compassionate tones. None of the wolves had ever seen a tape recorder before.

"Now then, no feeling sorry for him," said the King of the Wolves. "You all know the drill. We get down to the edge of the road, and at the first chance we tear him to pieces. That's all part of the great pattern of nature I was mentioning a moment ago."

"That'll take his mind off his earache," said one of the wolves with a fierce, sarcastic snarl.

As the sun set majestically in the west, Brighton, his cloak billowing around him like a private storm cloud, reached the great forest. It was like entering another world, for a mysterious twilight reigned

under the wide branches, a twilight without moon or stars. Tall, sombre pines looked down as if they feared the worst. But Brighton skated on, humming to himself. He was listening to the music of *The Noble Savage* and was waiting for one of the parts he liked best. Indeed, so busy was he humming and counting the beats that he did not notice a sudden wobble in his wheels. However, a moment after the wobble, his skates gave a terrible screech and he was pitched into the pine needles by the side of the road.

"Horrakapotchkin!" cried Brighton. "My poor skates!" (It was typical of this dancer that his first thought was for others.) However, his second thought was of the forest and the wolves that might be lurking there. It occurred to him that they might be tired of merino sheep, and would fancy a change of diet.

"Quick thought! Quick feet!" he said, quoting an old dancing proverb. He rushed around collecting a pile of firewood and pine cones, and then lit a good-sized fire there on the roadside. It was just as well he did, because when he looked up he saw the forest was alight with fiery red eyes. The wolves had arrived. They stole out of the forest and sat down on the edge of the firelight, staring at him very hard, all licking their lips in a meaningful way.

Brighton did not panic. Quietly, he rewound his tape recorder to the very beginning, and then

81

stood up coolly and began to do his exercises. A lesser dancer might have started off dancing straight away, but Brighton knew the greatest challenge of his life was ahead of him. He preferred to take things slowly and warm up properly in case he needed to do a few tricky steps before the night was out.

The wolves looked at each other uneasily. The king hesitated. There was something so tuneful about the music and so graceful about Brighton's dancing that he would have liked to watch it for a bit longer, but he knew he was part of nature's great plan, and must help his pack to tear Brighton to pieces. So he gave the order. "Charge!"

As one wolf the wolves ran towards Brighton, snarling and growling, but to their astonishment Brighton did not run away. No! He actually ran toward them and then leaped up in the air—up, up and right over them—his cloak streaming out behind him. It had the words HOOKYWALKER SCHOOL OF DRAMATIC ART painted on it. The wolves were going so fast that they could not stop themselves until they were well down the road. Brighton, meanwhile, landed with a heroic gesture, wheeled around, and then went on with his exercises, watching the wolves narrowly.

Once again, the wolves charged, and once again Brighton leaped. This time he jumped even higher, and the wolves couldn't help gasping in

admiration, much as they hated missing out on any prey.

"Right!" cried the King of the Wolves. "Let's run around him in ever-decreasing circles." (This was an old wolf trick.) "He'll soon be too giddy to jump." However, being a wolf and not used to classical ballet, the king didn't realize that a good dancer can spin on his toes without getting in the least bit giddy. Brighton spun until he was a mere blur and actually rose several inches in the air with the power of his rotation. It was the wolves who became giddy first; they stumbled over one another, ending up in a heap, with their red eyes all crossed. Finally, they struggled up with their tongues hanging out, but they had to wait for their eyes to get uncrossed again.

Seeing they were disabled for the moment by the wonder of his dancing, Brighton now gave up mere jumps and spins and began demonstrating his astonishing technique. Used as he was to dancing for animals, there was still a real challenge about touching the hearts of wolves. Besides, he knew he couldn't go on twirling and leaping high in the air all night. His very life depended on the quality of his dancing. He began with the first solo from *The Noble Savage*. Never in all his life, even at the School of Dramatic Art, had he been more graceful. First, he danced the loneliness of the Noble Savage, and the wolves (though they always traveled in a pack, and were never ever lonely) were so stirred that several of them pointed their noses into the air and howled in exact time to the music. It was most remarkable. Brighton now turned toward the wolves and began to express through dance his pleasure at seeing them. He made it very convincing. Some of the wolves began to wag their tails.

"He's really got something!" said the King of the Wolves. "This is high-class stuff." Of course, he said it in wolf language, but Brighton was good at reading the signs and became more poetic than ever before.

"Let me see," said the King of the Wolves, fascinated. "With a bit of practice I could manage an act like this myself. I always knew there was more to life than mere ravening. Come on! Let's give it a go!" The wolves began to point their paws and copy whatever movements Brighton made.

Seeing what they were about, Brighton began to encourage them by doing a very simple step and shouting instructions.

"You put your left paw in, you put your left paw out . . . ."

Of course, the wolves could not understand the words, but Brighton was very clever at mime and they caught on to the idea of things, dancing with great enthusiasm. Naturally, they were not as graceful as Brighton, but then they had not practiced for years as he had. Brighton could not help but be proud of them as they began a slow progress down the road back to the city, away from the forest and the sheep on the other side. The moon rose higher in the sky, and still Brighton danced, and the entranced wolves followed him, pointing their paws. It was very late at night when they entered the city once more. People going home from the cinema stared and shouted, and pointed (fingers, not toes). A lot of them joined in, either dancing or making music on musical instruments—banjos, trombones, combs—or anything that happened to be lying around.

In the School of Dramatic Art, wicked Antoine was just about to dance the very part Brighton usually danced when the sound of the procession made him hesitate. The audience, full of curiosity, left the theater. Outside was Brighton, swaying with weariness but still dancing, followed by twenty wolves, all dancing most beautifully by now, all in time and all very pleased with themselves, though, it must be admitted, all very hungry.

"Oh," cried the director of the School of Dramatic Art, rushing out to kiss Brighton on both cheeks. "What talent! What style! This will save the School of Dramatic Art from extinction."

"Send out for a supply of sausages," panted Brighton, "and write into the wolves' contracts that they will have not only sausages of the best quality, but that their names will appear in lights on top of the theater. After all, if they are dancing here every night, they won't be able to chase and worry sheep, will they?"

After this, there was peace for a long time, both in the city and out on the farms (where the sheep grew very fat and woolly). The School of Dramatic Art did wonderfully well. People came from miles around to see Brighton and his dancing wolves, and, of course—just as he had predicted—after dancing until late at night, the wolves were too weary to go out ravening sheep. Everyone was delighted (except for the jealous dancers, who just sulked and sizzled). Antoine, in particular, had such bad attacks of jealousy that it ruined his digestion and made his stomach rumble loudly, which forced him to abandon ballet altogether. However, Brighton, the wolves, the farmers, the director, and many other people, lived happily ever after in Hookywalker, that great city that people sometimes see looming out of the mist on the fringe of many fairy tales.

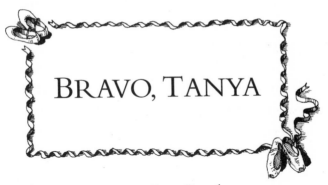

BRAVO, TANYA

Patricia Lee Gauch

Tiny Tanya loved to dance. She and her ballerina bear, Barbara, danced anywhere, any time. Sometimes they did their *pas de deux* in the meadow. Sometimes by the brook. Sometimes to music only they heard.

Tanya loved to dance so much that her mother sent her to dancing class with her sister, Elise. Barbara had to stay in her bag.

At the first class Tanya was very happy. She put on her slippers and her leotard, just like all the dancers. When they went to the *barre*, she did too. She walked just so, like a ballerina. And when Miss Bessinger said, "First position," Tanya already knew it. She knew second, fourth, and fifth, as well.

But when the woman with the comb in her hair began to play the piano, and Miss Bessinger clapped her hands and spoke at the same time,

"One, two, three, four. One, two, three, four," Tanya could not hear any music at all.

Clap, clap, clap, clap. "One, two, three, four," is what she heard. And so when Miss Bessinger said, "*Jeté*," Tanya was one *jeté* behind.

When Miss Bessinger said, "*Pirouette*," Tanya twirled into the girl with a ponytail. And when Miss Bessinger came up and whispered just to her, "ONE, TWO, THREE, FOUR!" when everyone was doing an *arabesque*, Tanya teetered and fell. This didn't feel like dancing at all.

Still, each Saturday Tanya took Barbara and went to class anyway.

By trying very hard, most of the time she kept in step for the *glissades*. She finally did an *arabesque* and even a *grand écart*.

Then one day when all of the parents came to visit and the dancers were all in a line doing *sauts de chat*, the piano was so loud, Miss Bessinger's counting was so loud, Tanya stopped short and the other dancers danced right into her.

"It's all right," she heard Miss Bessinger tell her mother later. "Not everyone is a dancer. She is a lovely child, and she is enjoying herself, and that is what matters."

So Tanya took Barbara and started home ahead of her mother and Elise. She wasn't a lovely child, and she wasn't enjoying herself. Not at all.

Down by the brook she stopped. She just

wanted to sit, but her ballerina bear, Barbara, didn't.
Barbara wanted to dance.

"Well, all right," Tanya said. And so they did
their *pas de deux* on the rocks by the brook.

And next to the waterfall where the brook came
from the hill.

And near the woods where the branches sang.

Then Barbara was the audience while Tanya
danced all alone in the meadow where she could
hear the music in the wind.

Tanya didn't even see the piano player with the

comb in her hair hiking across the field. And she didn't see her stop and watch with Barbara.

But when Tanya finally stopped dancing, she heard the clapping. It was a different kind from Miss Bessinger's. "Bravo," the piano player said.

Tanya was so surprised her cheeks grew pink. "You like the music here," the piano player said. "I do too." The sun made the lady's hair shine on top. "When I play the piano, sometimes I hear the wind. Sometimes I hear a storm. Sometimes I hear waves on a beach." Both Tanya and Barbara were surprised at that.

"Bravo again," she said, and smiling, she got up and hiked across the field.

The next Saturday Tanya tucked Barbara into her bag and went to dance class.

When Miss Bessinger said, "Stretch," Tanya stretched. When she said, first and second, fourth and fifth position, *plié* and *jeté*, Tanya did. She even did more than one *saut de chat*.

But when Miss Bessinger clapped—one, two, three, four, one, two, three, four—Tanya listened to the piano instead. She heard waves, a storm, and branches in the wind. And she danced.

"My goodness," Miss Bessinger said later. "What a little ballerina you are!"

When she left that day, Tanya smiled at the piano player with the comb in her hair as she walked across the floor.

Every Saturday Tanya went to dance class. Her ballerina bear, Barbara, went too. She went to the *barre* and she danced every step.

But Tanya and Barbara still liked best to dance a *pas de deux*, sometimes in the meadow, sometimes by the brook. Sometimes to music only they heard.

THE DOG STAR

Alison Prince

Gordon Bennett gave Patsy his paw and gazed at her through the brown hair that fell over his eyes. His name had come from what Patsy's grandad said when he first saw him as a puppy. "Gordon Bennett, what on earth is that?" Even then, Gordon Bennett had looked like a large, unravelling woolly, but he was Patsy's best friend and always understood how she felt.

"Dancing class this morning was awful," Patsy told him. "That beastly Camilla keeps calling me Fatsy."

Gordon Bennett put his head on Patsy's knee and looked sympathetic.

"I tried calling her Camel," Patsy went on, "but she just laughed and told me not to be silly. People are always laughing at me." Perhaps it was the way her headband tended to slip down over one eye, she thought. Camilla had long, dark hair that could be pinned into a proper dancer's bun, but Patsy's hair was more like a sort of haystack. And this morning Miss Silver had said, "Patsy, dear, do try to look *through* the wall, not at it." The trouble was, Patsy couldn't help thinking of the garbage cans and parked cars that she'd see if she really could look through it, and they weren't exactly poetic.

"I don't think I'll go to ballet next week," she told Gordon Bennett, and he sat up and gave her both paws, one in each hand. Patsy had been teaching him to dance. "Come on, then," she said, "let's waltz." And she soon felt better.

The following Saturday, after everyone had done their curtsy to Miss Silver, she said, "Before we start today, we need to plan our end-of-term show. So sit down, everyone." When they were all cross-legged on the floor, she went on, "I thought we'd call it *The Midnight Party*. Like in *Coppélia* when the toys come to life, you know!"

Patsy didn't know, but the others all nodded and smiled, except for Elvis, who looked as if he thought all that was kids' stuff. Elvis was the oldest and biggest in the class, and he was the only boy except for little Eric, who didn't really count.

"Each of you can choose your favorite toy," Miss Silver was saying, "and we'll make up a dance for whatever you are."

Camilla's hand was up at once. "I want to be a princess," she said. Miss Silver said a princess wasn't a toy, but Camilla said her Barbie doll had a princess outfit and that's what she was going to be. "I'll cry if I can't," she said, and started to cry straight away, just to prove that she could.

"All right," Miss Silver said quickly, "you're a princess. Who's next?"

"I'm an alien," said Elvis. "Kerpow, splut."

Miss Silver gazed at him doubtfully, but every-one said things like, "Wow!" and "Terrific!" They all thought Elvis was great. Camilla, who had stopped crying, had once boasted that he'd let her have a go at his Football Crazy video game, but nobody was sure if this was true.

"Couldn't you be a jack-in-the-box?" asked Miss Silver.

"Nah," said Elvis.

Miss Silver sighed and said, "Perhaps that would do for Eric."

Eric put his thumb in his mouth.

"He wants to be a spider, don't you, Eric?" said his sister, Jacqui.

Eric nodded.

A little desperately, Miss Silver said, "What about you, Patsy? What's your favorite toy?"

"My dog, really," said Patsy.

"A toy dog?" asked Miss Silver.

"No, he's real. Gordon Bennett."

"I beg your pardon?"

"Gordon Bennett. That's his name." People were starting to giggle.

Debbie said she wouldn't mind being a plastic duck. Miss Silver gave another sigh. "I'll have to put my thinking cap on," she said, and clapped her hands for them all to stand up and go to the *barre*.

The next Saturday, Miss Silver read aloud from a piece of paper what everyone had to be. Most of the girls were dolls—Russian and Indian and

Spanish and Chinese—except for Camilla, who of course was a princess, and the beginners, who had to be the children who woke up and watched. Elvis was an alien from a story in a book; Eric was a spider; and Patsy was the Dog Star, who looked in through the window and then did a dawn dance to tell everyone the revels had to end. "You'll have to do lots of running about, sending people back to their places," said Miss Silver. "You'll like that, won't you?"

Patsy nodded, but the idea filled her with terror. "Why does this Dog Star have to run about?" she asked. She'd be bound to trip over something.

"Because it's the last star in the sky," Miss Silver explained. "It's like a sheepdog, making sure all the others have gone to bed before the sun comes up. When your dance ends, we'll have a hoop covered with red tissue paper for the sun, and somebody can bring it slowly up from behind the piano. It'll look lovely."

Afterward, Patsy heard Camilla say to Donna, who was a teddy bear, "I think you should have been the Dog Star, and Fatsy could do the paper hoop. She's so hopeless."

Gordon Bennett gave Patsy's nose an affectionate lick when she told him this, but it took a lot of waltzing before she felt better. Her mother was firm and encouraging. "You'll be marvelous, darling, I know you will," she said. "I'm really looking forward to it." She was helping with the costumes, and had made Patsy a brown headband with big furry ears on it, and a pair of shaggy trousers contrived from an old pair of tights and a lot of rug wool. Because Patsy was a star of the night as well as being doggy, she had a black, spangly top over the furry trousers—and furry mitts for paws. It all made her feel very hot. And she had to manage a star on a stick as well.

The day of the performance came. Peeping from behind the curtain, Patsy could see her mother sitting in the third row with Patsy's baby brother Allan, on her knee and Grandad beside her. Patsy wondered what they'd done with Gordon Bennett. (He couldn't be left alone in the house, because he ate everything.) She soon found out. When Mrs. Abercrombie struck up the opening music on the piano, everyone could hear Gordon Bennett howling outside, where he had been tied to the railings. As the toys did their waking-up dance, he howled even louder. Patsy saw her mother hand Allan to Grandad and tiptoe out. She came back with Gordon Bennett and made him sit down in the aisle beside her, then retrieved Allan, who was starting to howl as well.

Meanwhile, *The Midnight Party* was going fairly well. Eric got in a muddle with his spider dance and had to be rescued by Miss Silver, but Elvis was

a wonderful alien in a costume that had taken a roll
and a half of baking foil. He had a cycle-helmet
headdress with two yellow tennis balls on springs,
and did amazing things with his knees.

As Mrs. Abercrombie's husband raised the paper-
hoop sun from behind the piano, Patsy made her
entrance and started her dance. Unfortunately, she
tripped over Camilla's crown and got it stuck on
her foot, but she ignored the giggles and came to
the front of the stage to begin the final sleepy
waltz. It was then that Gordon Bennett realized
who she was. Before Patsy's mom could grab his

leash, he leapt up onto the stage, sat down in front of the Dog Star and offered a paw.

"Go away!" Patsy muttered, and went on dancing. Her headband with the floppy ears had slipped over her eyes, and she had to keep her nose in the air to see where she was going. When she stopped for a moment to push it up, Gordon Bennett sat up in front of her and offered both paws. He wanted to dance. The audience was falling off its chairs with laughter.

"Oh, all right," said Patsy in desperation. She took Gordon Bennett's paws and he joined her in the waltz. He wasn't very good at it yet, and to make things worse, Patsy could feel her rug-woolly tights starting to slither down. She did her best to look through the wall like Miss Silver was always telling them, but people wouldn't stop laughing. As the music ended, she and Gordon Bennett stood hand in paw under the risen paper sun. Patsy's star drooped at the end of its stick, which had somehow become bent, and her furry tights had fallen around her ankles.

The applause was tumultuous, but when the curtains rattled shut, Camilla said furiously, "You ruined everything! And just look at my crown—it's squashed flat!"

Miss Silver gave Patsy a kiss and said, "You kept going, that's the main thing. Well done." And they all took another curtain call, Gordon Bennett included.

A few days later, Elvis came around to Patsy's house with his Football Crazy video game and a copy of the local paper.

"Seen this?" he asked. There was a big photo of Patsy and Gordon Bennett dancing, under a headline: STARS OF THE SHOW. Below that was a long column which said among other things that Patsy had a wonderful comic talent. Most people's names were spelled wrong, and Camilla came out as Vanilla, as if she were a kind of ice cream.

"Dead brill," said Elvis. "You wanna have a go at Football Crazy?"

Dancing classes were okay after that. Patsy didn't care any more about what Camilla-Vanilla said. She was too busy teaching Gordon Bennett how to tango.

BOYS DON'T DO BALLET— DO THEY?

Vivian French

"Whoops!" Jenny staggered as she pulled herself around the edge of the kitchen table on pointe. It didn't matter that she was really only balancing on the rubber edges of her school shoes. Inside her head she was pirouetting around and around a darkened stage with one silvery spotlight shining down on her gleaming dark hair . . . .

"JENNY!" Jenny's mom was standing in the kitchen doorway. "How many times do I have to tell you NOT to do that to your shoes? You'll RUIN them!"

Jenny gave her mom a guilty grin. "Sorry," she said, and she hopped into first position.

"Heels together . . . feet in a line. Look, Mom! Madam Anna says I have a wonderful turnout!"

"Madam Anna also says that you're still much too young to go on pointe," Mom said.

Jenny made a face. "I'm not MUCH too young."

"H'mph." Mom opened a drawer and slung a handful of knives and forks on the table. "Here—dance around and set the table for four for supper."

"Four? Who's coming?" Usually it was only Jenny and her mom.

Mom handed Jenny the salt and pepper. "Another ballet fan," she said. "I was hanging out the laundry and I got talking to the new people next door. Mrs. Davis told me that her youngest child—Christy, I think she said—really loves ballet. I said you went to Madam Anna's classes, and it ended up with me asking them in for supper."

"How old is she?" Jenny asked. "Has she done classes before? She could come with me. I'd look after her—I can show her all the positions. Madam Anna says I'm very good at looking after the little ones. I always tie their ribbons for them."

"I don't think you'll need to do that for Christy," Mom said. "He's a boy."

Jenny stared at her mom.

"A BOY? But boys don't do ballet!"

"Of course they do," Mom said. "What about Fritz in *The Nutcracker*? And Romeo? And—"

"I didn't mean THAT," Jenny said. "I meant, they don't do ballet at Madam Anna's. Well—only the very little boys, and they run around being silly."

Mom began to laugh. "Jenny! How do you think male dancers ever got started? They went to classes, just like you!"

Jenny shook her head. "But I don't WANT boys in our class. They'd spoil it. I know they would."

Mom was about to say something else when there was a loud RING! at the front door.

"There they are! Run and open the door, Jenny."

"Do I have to?" Jenny asked.

"Yes!" said Mom. "And hurry up!"

Jenny walked as slowly as she dared to the front door. She could feel Mom hoping that she would be friendly and nice, but she didn't want to be. She and her friends had been going to Madam Anna's for almost as long as she could remember. They had secrets and whispered together and boasted about how Madam Anna said that they were her best class ever. A boy would just get in the way. He wouldn't know what to do. He'd be silly, and rush around shouting, like the little boys. And—Jenny suddenly felt more cheerful—where would he change his clothes? The little boys hopped about in their underwear, but there was nowhere for older boys ... she was almost sure of it. As she opened the door she smiled a sorry-but-it's-no-good smile.

"Hello," she said to the neat little woman and the boy on the doorstep. "Do come in. I'm Jenny, but it won't be any good Christy coming to my ballet class because we don't have anywhere for boys to change their clothes." And she waved them inside.

Mrs. Davis looked a little surprised as she walked down the hall into the kitchen. Christy stopped on the doormat. "It doesn't matter about a place to change," he said cheerfully to Jenny. "I always went to class in my tights anyway. I only need to change my shoes. What level are you at? Are you on pointe yet?"

Jenny stared at him. He had a round face with bright red cheeks, and his eyes were very blue. He wasn't exactly fat, but he certainly wasn't thin, and he was only just as tall as she was. He didn't look in the least like any of the pictures of famous dancers she had pinned up in her bedroom. They were thin, and pale, with bony noses and high cheekbones. Christy looked like—Jenny scratched her nose and thought about it. What *did* he look like? Then she realized. Christy looked just like an ordinary boy. And all the ordinary boys Jenny knew liked football, or roller blades, or messing about in the park. They didn't EVER do ballet.

Christy was staring now, but he was still smiling. "Don't you speak?" he asked Jenny.

"When I want to," she said in her most hoity-toity voice, and ran into the kitchen where Mrs. Davis and Mom were sitting and chatting. Christy came after her, and sat himself down —without waiting to be asked.

"Hi!" he said to Mom, and he beamed his red-cheeked smile. Jenny scowled.

The supper party was not a success. At least, Jenny didn't think so. Mom enjoyed herself, and Mrs. Davis talked a great deal, and Christy ate a lot and answered all Mom's questions about school and ballet . . . but Jenny just wanted them to go away. She put her head right down while she was eating, and afterward she went to sit at the other end of the room from the others. She didn't want to know that Christy was going to be in her class at school. She didn't want to know that he had won a prize for dancing in a competition. And she *definitely* didn't want to know that Mrs. Davis had already spoken to Madam Anna and that Christy was going to come to her class the very next day.

"That's lovely," said Mom as Mrs. Davis and Christy got ready to go. "Isn't it, Jenny?"

Jenny made a snorting sort of noise.

"Maybe we could share dropping off and picking up," said Mrs. Davis, and Mom nodded. "I'd be delighted."

After Mrs. Davis and Christy had gone, Mom began to wash up. "Jenny," she said, "why were you so rude?"

Jenny wriggled. "I didn't mean to be," she said.

"Well," said Mom, "you were—very. Now, tomorrow Mrs. Davis is taking you to ballet, and I want you to be very helpful and look after Christy. Just think how you would feel if you were going to a new class and didn't know anyone."

Jenny wriggled some more. "But what will my friends say?"

"It doesn't matter what they say," Mom said.

Jenny sighed. Obviously Mom didn't understand at all.

Mrs. Davis knocked on the door the next day at a quarter to four. For the first time in her life Jenny wasn't looking forward to ballet class, and she wasn't ready. Mom scooped up her leotard and pink tights and pushed them into her bag.

"Come on, Jenny," she said, and she walked with Jenny to Mrs. Davis's car. Christy was already sitting in the back, wearing a striped sweater and baggy green trousers. Jenny sniffed as she got in beside him.

"I thought you said you always wore your tights to class," she said. "You can't do ballet in baggy trousers. Madam Anna likes us all to be very neat and tidy."

"It's okay." Christy said. "I've got tights on underneath." And he waved cheerfully to Jenny's Mom as they drove away.

It wasn't a long drive to the church hall where Madam Anna held her classes, but it seemed very long indeed to Jenny. She looked out of the window all the way so that she didn't have to talk to Christy. She invented conversations with her friends inside her head. "No, I know I came with him, but I couldn't help it." "Poor Jenny—having to come with a boy!" "A BOY—isn't it awful?" "I expect Madam Anna will put him in the little ones' class." "Boys NEVER know what to do. Fancy your mom telling you to look after him!" By the time Mrs. Davis stopped the car Jenny was feeling very sorry for herself, and she was quite certain that all her friends would feel sorry for her, too. She grabbed her bag and jumped out of the car, rushing to tell them. As she ran, her tights flopped out of her bag and tangled around her legs . . . and Jenny fell flat on her face.

"JENNY?"

Jenny scrambled up, and stared. Madam Anna—MADAM ANNA!—was right in front of her.

Jenny dropped her bag and tried to make her greeting curtsy, but as she said, "Good evening, Madam Anna," she wobbled and slipped sideways. Her face burned bright red as she stood up again.

"Jenny dear," Madam Anna said, "a ballerina does not arrive anywhere in a scrabble and a dash. Now, pick up your tights, and go inside and wash your hands and face."

Jenny grabbed her bag and her tights and hurried through the door. Her eyes were stinging with angry tears, and her hands and knees were hurting too. It was all that HORRIBLE boy's fault, she told herself. She had NEVER fallen over before. It HAD to be his fault. And she stamped into the changing room and flung herself down on a bench.

"Jenny! Jenny! Guess what! Guess!" Daisy and Sara and Edna and all her other friends were jumping up and down in excitement. "Guess what! There's a famous ballerina coming today to see Madam Anna! And guess what else! Her little boy is coming to join *our* class! Unless he's too good, of course, and then he'll go up to the seniors. But a *real* ballerina! She danced with the Royal Ballet, and she was Swanhilda in *Coppélia* and Madam Anna says she was an absolute rave!"

Jenny didn't move. She sat on the bench and said nothing at all. The other girls fussed and twittered around her, straightening their tights and smoothing their hair, but Jenny sat still—and thought.

It must be Mrs. Davis! Mrs. Davis—Christy's mom—was a real ballerina! And she, Jenny—Madam Anna's star dancer—had been rude to her! Had run away from her car! Had been horrid to Christy! Jenny felt as if a whirlwind was rushing about in her head. How would she ever look at Madam Anna again? Oh—if only she could turn time back . . . .

"Jenny! Jenny! Why aren't you getting ready?" Daisy was peering at her.

"Your face is dirty," Edna said. "What have you been doing?"

"I fell over," Jenny said. "I fell over on my way in." She didn't say she had been running away from the famous ballerina, but she felt her face grow hot as she thought about it. She got up and went to wash her hands.

"Did you see Madam Anna?" Sarah asked. "She's waiting outside—this ballerina must be VERY special!"

What do you think her boy will be like?" Edna did a *pirouette*.

"I expect he'll want to dance with me," Daisy said, and she smiled at herself in the mirror. Daisy was very pretty, and she was always popular with the boys at school.

"No, he won't," said Sarah. "He'll want to dance with Jenny. She's much the best dancer."

"He'll have to take turns," said Edna. "Or it won't be fair."

"Maybe now one boy's come, lots of others will too," said Gillie.

"Maybe," Daisy said, still gazing at herself in the mirror, "maybe we'll do lifts!"

"WOW!" breathed Edna and Sarah and Gillie.

Jenny, slowly pulling on her tights, felt worse and worse. It sounded as if all the other girls *liked*

112

the idea of Christy joining the class . . . as if they *wanted* boys to join in. She wriggled into her leotard, and put on her satin slippers.

"You're being very quiet," Edna told Jenny as she tied her ribbons. "What's the matter?"

"Nothing," Jenny said. She was just smoothing her hair when Madam Anna put her head around the door.

"Girls? Girls—come and meet Tara Talliori, formerly prima ballerina of the Royal Ballet. And you must welcome her son, already a dedicated dancer. Now remember—your VERY best curtsies, IF you please."

Daisy and Sara and Edna and the other girls squeaked and giggled their way out into the hall. Jenny took a deep breath, and followed them . . . .

Madam Anna was standing on the platform at the end of the hall. Beside her was Mrs. Davis, and beside Mrs. Davis was Christy, neatly dressed in a white T-shirt, black tights, and ballet shoes. To Jenny's amazement she saw that Christy

was blushing—a deep, fiery red creeping up over his face. He looked very uncomfortable indeed, and Jenny found herself feeling sorry for him.

"It must be *horrible* being up there in front of everybody," she thought, and as she felt more and more sorry for Christy she wished even more that she had been nicer to him.

"Girls," Madam Anna said, "we are very lucky this evening. Tara Talliori is going to lead us in our greeting curtsy, and then she will take the class—just for today. I hope you will all be MOST polite and do EXACTLY as she tells you." She turned and smiled at Tara Talliori, and Tara Talliori nodded back.

"Perhaps Christy could join the other students?" Tara—or Mrs. Davis—asked, and Christy jumped down from the platform so quickly that Jenny was certain he had been longing and longing to get away. He hurried down the hall and came to stand next to Jenny, but he didn't look at her.

Jenny swallowed. There was an uncomfortable feeling in her throat. She had ignored him all the way to ballet class; was he going to do the same to her now?

"Are we ready?" Madam Anna called out, and she held out her arms. Tara Talliori did the same, and all the girls copied her. Christy put his hands on his waist.

"One, two, three—and DOWN," said Madam Anna . . . and down they all sank—all except Christy. Christy bowed a low deep bow, and he bowed straight at Jenny . . . and winked at her . . . and wobbled . . . and fell over.

As he scrambled up both he and Jenny began to laugh. Even when Madam Anna frowned at them they couldn't stop, and Daisy and Edna and Sarah and all the other girls began to laugh, too . . . Tara Talliori laughed the loudest of all. Even Madam Anna seemed to be smiling.

As the noise died down Tara Talliori walked over to the piano. "Do you mind if I play?" she asked, and before the pianist could answer, she began to play a wild and toe-tapping polka.

"Take your partners!" she called out. "Let's begin with a warm-up! Remember your posture—and listen to the music!"

There was a moment's complete silence. No class of Madam Anna's had ever begun with a polka .... Then Edna and Sarah grabbed each other's hands and began to hop and skip in circles.

Jenny hesitated, and then looked sideways at Christy. He was looking at her, and he took her hand as if it were the most ordinary thing in the world. As they jumped and hopped around the room, it was as if they had always been friends. Jenny smiled to herself. Maybe boys doing ballet wasn't such a bad thing after all ....

And when she and Christy bounced past Madam Anna, and Madam Anna clapped her hands, Jenny was sure of it.

ANNA'S SHOES

Penny Speller

A nna pulled at the edges of her shoes to stretch them and squeezed her feet in.

"This is silly," said her mother. "Your feet must be agony and it can't be doing them any good to be cramped inside those shoes."

"They're okay," said Anna. She sat with her back to her mom as she tied the ribbons. Her mom started pulling at her hair with the hair brush.

"Ouch! You're hurting," she grumbled.

"We wouldn't be so late if you didn't have to spend so long trying to cram your feet into a tiny pair of shoes."

Anna elbowed her sneakers out of sight under a nearby chair. They were new and so much bigger than her old ballet shoes. The ballet shoes were soft and used to be pink, but they were turning crinkly and gray. She could see the bulges of her big toes underneath the leather and they pinched across the top of her foot where they were too tight.

"There's nothing wrong with my shoes," Anna said. She jumped up and shuffled off toward the dance studio for her class.

The Dorothy Russell Academy of Dance was well known for the achievements of its pupils. Dorothy Russell was proud of the high examination marks that her dancers always gained and Anna was one of her star pupils. She frowned to see her enter the studio late.

"Come along, dear, we've a lot to get through this morning."

"Sorry, Mrs. Russell," Anna muttered as she joined the other girls.

"We must practice the entire set piece for your exam—and the exercises," she said. "Warm-ups first —at the *barre* I think."

The girls took their places.

"*Pliés* first," Mrs. Russell announced. "With the music: and one and two and three. Very good, Hazel; keep your back straighter, Eleanor; smile, Anna, you look like you're in pain."

Anna forced a smile onto her face, but it was difficult. Her feet really did hurt and it was hard to balance when she had to keep her toes scrunched up. Mrs. Russell stared at her.

"I don't know what it is," she said, "but your form does seem to be slipping at the moment,

Anna. Your knees are tight, your legs are wobbling about all over the place and your shoulders are hunched. You're surely not nervous about the exam?"

"A bit," Anna said. She was glad to be given an excuse for her dancing and not to have to think one up for herself. "But I know I'll be all right on the day," she added, looking down at her shoes. "I absolutely know it."

"Not if you don't relax a bit," said Mrs. Russell. "You know the steps, you just need to relax. Still, at least you have confidence. Now, into the center, girls, let's practice our set piece. One at a time."

Anna watched while Claire and Hazel went

through the dance. The girls always sat in silence during these lessons. She pulled her feet a little way out of her shoes and wiggled her toes to let them stretch about.

Then it was her turn.

The dance started well and Anna found that when she thought about the steps and the music she forgot about her feet hurting. This was how she loved to dance, thinking about nothing else but how good it felt to be in control of her body and moving to the music. The dance ended with an *atttude*. Anna had held the position like a statue many times before, but she had been finding it increasingly difficult. As soon as the music stopped she became aware of her scrunched, pinched, aching feet. Her leg wobbled and Anna fell with a heavy thud onto the wooden floor.

"Anna, that is not going to get the Distinction that we know you deserve," said Mrs. Russell.

Anna sat. Now her legs and her feet hurt and, before she could stop herself, she burst into tears.

"Let me see. Are you hurt?" Mrs. Russell put an arm around Anna's shoulders.

"I'm all right," she sniffed. She tried to stand up but Mrs. Russell put her other arm out to stop her.

"Just a minute," she said. "Let me have a look at those shoes."

Anna felt her cheeks blush red under her tears. Mrs. Russell looked at Anna's feet and then pulled off the shoes. There were dents in her skin where they had been pinching.

"Anna, how long have you had these shoes?" Mrs. Russell asked.

"Mom bought them for me for my Grade One exam," Anna admitted. "When I got my first Distinction."

"But that was over a year ago," said Mrs. Russell. "Didn't you remind her that you needed new ones?"

"I don't need new ones," Anna sobbed. "I need these ones." She looked down at the limp, empty shoes on the studio floor.

"But why?" Mrs. Russell asked. "They're only ballet shoes."

Anna picked up the shoes.

"Because if I wear these shoes, I'll get a Distinction," she said. "They did it before."

Mrs. Russell went over to a cupboard in the corner of the studio. She unlocked it with a small brass key and lifted out an old shoebox held together with a rubber band.

"Gather round, girls, I want to show you something."

Inside the box was a collection of old ballet shoes: some satin, some leather. They were different sizes and colors, but they were all crinkly and faded like Anna's and smelt of old socks. Mrs. Russell held up the tiniest pair. They were almost as thin as paper.

"These were my first ballet shoes," she said. "When I was five. And these—" she held up a faded red pair of pointe shoes—"I wore the first time I danced on stage. And these—" they were white; "I wore the last time I danced for an audience before I retired to open my Academy. Every pair has its own story to tell."

Anna looked at all the different shoes lying in

the old box, never to be worn again. They made her feel sad and she held on tight to her own pair. Then she looked at Mrs. Russell. Her hair was gray and her face was all wrinkly, but when she smiled her eyes sparkled like new.

"You see, Anna," she said, "it's not the shoes that pass the exam, it's you."

"But I dance better in these shoes," said Anna.

"You dance better because you practice." Mrs. Russell looked serious. "Treasure your old shoes, but buy some new ones to wear. Until then I'll find you a pair to borrow."

Anna put her old shoes down at the side of the studio and put on the borrowed pair. Her feet felt comfortable at last but they didn't look like her own feet any more. She tried a few steps, then a few more. They still didn't look right. Then Anna lifted her head and stopped looking at the strange shoes. Suddenly it didn't seem to matter that she was wearing them. Her feet felt as if they could move at last. She smiled as she held herself in a perfect *attitude* without wobbling.

"You see?" Mrs. Russell smiled and clapped her hands. "I knew you could do it. Now let's see you do the set piece properly."

On the day of the exam, Anna took two pairs of shoes into the studio. One pair she wore for the first time. The smooth pink leather looked like new skin and Anna's feet felt light and free inside them. The other pair sat on top of the piano where Anna could see them. They no longer looked pink, the stitches were coming out and anyone else might have thrown them away. But not Anna. She always kept her precious first pair of ballet shoes safely in an old shoebox.

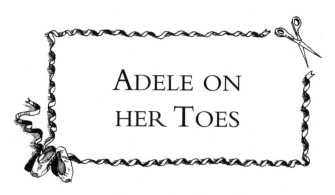

ADELE ON HER TOES

Patricia Reilly Giff

December 21

The whole school was having a party. Kids were sliding around in the hall chewing hard ribbon candy. Streamers and balloons were everywhere.

Almost the whole school was having a party. But not my classroom. My classroom was reading compositions aloud: WHAT I LOVE TO DO MOST IN THE WORLD. John Englehart wasn't listening. He was shaking his head around at me. With all that hair, he looked like a boar.

I tried to pay attention to the compositions. I knew what I wanted to do most. I wanted to be a ballerina. A ballerina in a pink tutu. I wanted to be up on my toes, with a long skinny neck and a bun on the back of my head.

But I was in trouble. I had forgotten to write
the composition. And even if I had written it, John
Englehart would have laughed himself silly: Adele
Redfern with a long neck and a bun!

That boar-head John Englehart. At lunch, he
had even grabbed my salami sandwich and twirled
it around, snuffling at it.

Disgusting.

But now, here it was. Trouble. Mrs. Holstein
pointed one long finger at me. "Adele," she said.
"Please come up to the front and read what you've
written."

What luck. The door was open. Kids were
exploding out of the rest of the rooms calling
"Happy Holidays!" and I was ready to read a blank
piece of paper. I was ready to make up the whole
thing as I went along.

I made it up slowly. My hands were shaking so it looked as if the paper was traveling through a wind storm. I made it up in a low voice. It was a good thing John Englehart was sitting on the other side of the room. He'd have needed a hearing aid like my mother's Aunt Gertie to know what I was saying.

After a few seconds I couldn't think of anything more to make up about my beautiful ballet outfits. So I told about my ballet lessons. I told about *pirouettes* and *bourées* and *arabesques*. It was all I could remember. I had taken only four lessons . . . and we hadn't even gotten to any of that stuff. The ballet teacher had moved away to start a worm farm.

But Mrs. Holstein was nodding. She was smiling. "Adele," she said. "You may join the winter ballet group at my church. It starts in two weeks."

"But . . ." I began.

The bell rang. Mrs. Holstein was finished with us. Mary, Emma, and I slid out to the hall. John Englehart slid after us, snorting. His hair was dangling in his eyes.

We paid no attention.

"You love to *pirouette*?" Mary asked me, rolling her eyes.

"Well . . ."

"You love to *bourée*?" Emma said.

I bit my lip.

"Happy Holidays," they said.

Downstairs my mother was making Christmas cookies. My baby brother, Ignot, was eating the sprinkles.

I was upstairs in the guest room. I was too sad to eat cookies. I was counting the days. What would Mrs. Holstein say when she found out I wasn't a ballerina?

What would she say if she knew I had lied?

I needed a studio to practice in. I looked around. A mirror stood in one corner. I could see my whole self. Fat cheeks, square teeth with a big space in the middle.

"You are not a hippopotamus, Adele," I told myself. "You are a ballerina."

I ran my hand along the bed railing. It was a perfect *barre*. I began to shove the dresser into the corner.

A moment later my mother was at the door. She had Ignot in one arm. She was holding a piece of ribbon candy. "The best," she said. She broke off a piece for me. "The last one, too bad."

"I'm doing ballet," I said. I reached for Ignot and swooped him up into my arms. He began to chew on my sleeve.

My mother tucked a lock of hair behind one ear and looked around at the karate posters on the wall. I had tacked them up in September.

"It was because of John Englehart," I told her. "I was trying to get courage."

My mother ran her foot over the bowling-ball lines I had painted on the floor last summer. "What next?" she said, but she was smiling.

I kept patting Ignot's warm back. "It would be nice to be a star," I said. "Nobody in this family has ever been famous."

My mother shook her head. "I guess not." She snapped her fingers. "That reminds me. The guest room. Nana is coming for Christmas. Today. Tomorrow. Any minute."

Ignot eased his teeth from my elbow. I opened my mouth. Nana, my grandmother: Adele Ignot. I nodded. Nana was famous. Almost famous, anyway. She had won a contest for counting beans in a jar; she had walked across New York State in a day; and she had eaten two apple pies in one sitting. We even had the newspaper clippings to prove it.

"I hope she won't mind karate posters and bowling-ball lines." My mother smiled around the candy.

"Never." I put my arms around her. "Happy Holidays," I said.

My mother nodded. "When Nana comes, the best things happen."

December 23

I raced down the street. I banged into the library. "Books," I told Mrs. Green. "Ballet books, please."

I didn't have a minute to waste. I had to learn *arabesques*. I had to learn *bourées*. I had to learn everything.

I rushed back home and opened one of the books on the hall floor. I looked at the pictures. Foot positions. Arm positions.

Good grief. There was a lot to learn in two weeks.

I turned to the middle of the book. *Pas de chat.* The step of a cat. "Jump like a cat. Dart like a cat," said the book.

I jumped and darted down the hall.

I took quick peeks in the mirror as I passed the guest-room door. "You are not a hippopotamus, Adele," I said, gritting my teeth.

And then I heard the car drive up.

I jumped like a cat to the guest-room window. Nana's purple van was half-way up the kerb. The van was her whole house. She lived in it in between visiting aunts and cousins and grandchildren. She drove it to the beach in winters and the mountains in summers. And right now she unfolded herself out of the purple door. She smushed down her velvet hat against the wind. She tossed her ball-fringe scarf around her neck.

My mother stood outside in the snow holding Ignot. "Wave to Nana," she was saying.

Ignot wasn't answering. He was chewing on her look-like-fur collar.

I leaned out of the window. "Hey, Nana," I yelled.

Nana looked up. "Hey, Adele," she yelled back.

Ignot said his first words. I think they were his first—it was amazing. The words sounded like "Happy Holidays."

Nana had four plaid suitcases, a statue of her dead dog, Ivan the Terrible, and a round ball with a strange bubbly pink liquid swirling around inside. I reached for the ball, and followed Nana upstairs, rolling it around in my hands.

"Please don't drop that, Adele," my mother

said, looking at the new plaid carpet on our stairs.

"She won't," said Nana.

"Is it a crystal ball?" I asked.

"A globe," said Nana.

"Is it magic?" I kept my fingers crossed. I didn't believe in magic. But I needed something. I needed anything. I needed to become a ballerina fast.

It was the only way to cross out the lie I had told.

"There's something for you," Nana was saying at the same time. "A pink package. A blue one for Ignot. And red for your mother and father."

"I love pink," I said.

"I love red," said my mother.

"Put them under the tree, Gorgeous," said Nana.

We spent the rest of the day "settling Nana in." That's what she called it. Suitcases opened. Velvet dresses unpacked. Lace collars on the dresser. Shoes with diamonds. Shoes with sharp black heels. Shoes with wrap-around straps up the legs like snakes.

"From my acting days," said Nana.

We put the globe in the middle of the floor. "It needs space," said Nana. "It needs to settle in."

December 24

I was having a bad dream. It was all about telling lies. It was all about John Englehart, the wild boar.

I opened my eyes. It was morning. I threw on my robe and went down the hall.

Nana was wearing a robe too. It was gold with green sprinkles.

"Tell me the story of your life in a minute," said Nana.

I opened my mouth. I told her about wanting to be a ballerina with a long neck and a bun on my head. I could hear my mother blasting the oven door shut with the turkey inside.

I told her about Mrs. Holstein's winter ballet group. Outside I could hear my father hammering up the decorations. Three wire reindeer and a wooden Santa Claus.

I told her John Englehart was always laughing at me and making boar faces. I could hear Ignot chomping on his crib.

I told her I looked like a hippopotamus.

I didn't tell her about the composition and the lie.

"Hmm," Nana was saying. "I think we can fix all that."

"I forgot about foot positions and arm positions," I said. "And *pas de chat*."

"Don't worry," said Nana. "Look into the globe."

"We can fix all of it?" I asked. "It must be magic."

"Nonsense," said Nana. "You just need to believe."

"Happy Holidays," I said.

It was morning, almost morning. It was still dark outside, except for the patches of snow in the streetlight.

I could see the wire reindeer and the Santa Claus.

"It's too early for presents," my father said. "It's the middle of the night."

Nana appeared in the hall. She was wearing a turban with stars. "Present time," she sang.

I could hear Ignot in his crib. "Happyhappyhappyhap . . . ."

And my mother groaning. "I just got to bed," she said.

We came downstairs. Skillions of presents under the tree. I loved looking at them. Ignot loved chewing on them.

I picked up Nana's pink package. Inside were ballet slippers. Soft, pink, beautiful.

I tried them on. The perfect fit for a hippopotamus.

Ignot had teething rings. Piles of them.

And Mother and Father had ribbon candy. Piles of that too.

After breakfast, I went up to the guest room. I sat on the dresser, my feet dangling. "How did you know what we wanted?" I asked. "Ballet shoes are good . . . ."

"But not enough," said Nana. "Right?"

She pointed to the globe on the floor. I slid off the dresser. Together we stared at it. I could feel Nana's stiff yellow curls against my face. She pressed her nose against the glass. "This is how you do it," she said.

I brought my eyes up close . . . so close they were almost crossed. What could I see? Pink. Bubbles shooting around.

"What do you see?" Nana asked.

"Streams of . . . a glow."

"Nothing else?" Nana polished the ball with the edge of her gold robe. "Lean closer," she said. "Think about ballet."

She tapped the globe. The streams swirled. I thought about ballet. I thought about a pink tutu and a bun. I thought about the ballet slippers, and I could almost . . . not quite . . .

"Good grief!" I scrambled back.

"What? What?" asked Nana.

"A boar's head," I said. "John Englehart."

"Nonsense," said Nana.

December 26

Nana sat me in front of the mirror. She began to work with the scissors.

At the same time she showed me foot positions. Feet together. Feet forward. Feet backward.

Snip snip.

And arm positions. Arms out. Arms up.

Snip snip.

I had bangs.

Snip snip.

The ends of my hair were even and straight.

Nana rustled through one of the suitcases. Up went the hair into a ponytail ring. "Enough for a bun when you want to be elegant," said Nana. "For when you're practicing foot positions and arm positions a hundred times."

137

I looked into the globe.

I could almost see my face in the bubbles.

Somehow the hippopotamus was gone.

What was left was . . .

a not bad girl.

I sighed. Still a girl who had told a lie.

December 27

Nana was snipping with the scissors again.

Snip snip . . .

on her old pink tulle petticoat.

Snip snip . . .

on her old bedroom curtains.

"Good thing I bring everything with me," she said, and frowned. "Dash down to the store. Bring me back a spool of pink thread."

On the way to the store I twirled around the telephone poles. I practiced *pirouettes* to stay warm.

I stopped for the pink thread. "It's for a tutu," I told Mrs. Leahy.

She rustled through the drawers of thread for the right color. "You're looking perky," she said.

Going back I did *pas de chat*. I darted and jumped past John Englehart's house. I was so busy with the darting I forgot and waved to him.

He didn't wave back, of course.

I slipped on a puddle with a topping of ice. I was ready to freeze to death.

I let myself in the back door with my teeth chattering. Ignot crawled over to give me a friendly bite on my boots. My mother asked, "How's the ballet?"

I sighed. "Horrible."

January 1

It was a whole new year. We ate a huge ham for dinner and then Nana packed up. "I'm off," she said, "to the seashore."

"Don't go," I said. I could hardly talk. I was going to turn into a hippopotamus again. I would never be a ballet star.

I helped Nana pack. She saw that I was ready to cry. "I'll leave you the globe," she said. "I'll be back for your birthday in March. You can put on a ballet for me."

I nodded.

"Remember what I said." Nana took my chin in her hand. "You just have to believe in yourself."

"I think I believe in the globe," I said.

Nana just laughed.

Downstairs I held Ignot. We waved from the window.

"Happyhappyhappyhap," said Ignot, smiling at me.

I patted the globe. At the last minute I leaned out of the window. "I told a lie," I called.

It was too late. The purple van turned the corner. Nana was gone.

My mother helped with the bun on my head. I carried the pink tutu over my arm and the globe bulging out of my pocket.

My teeth were chattering again. But not from the cold. I kept patting the globe. I needed it to make me brave.

Mrs. Holstein was waiting in the hallway of her church. "Just in time, Adele," she said.

I opened my mouth. "I may not be so good at ballet," I said. I could hear a bunch of kids in the other room.

"I'll teach you," said Mrs. Holstein. "You just need to believe you can do it."

I nodded. I followed her inside. I swallowed. Thirty kids were there. They were leaning against a *barre*. They were doing foot positions. They were doing arm positions. They were darting and jumping and . . .

They looked like beginners. They looked just like me.

Mrs. Holstein was smiling. "See."

I darted and jumped. I jumped right into John Englehart with his dangling hair and his wild-boar face.

Mrs. Holstein began to teach us *bourées*.

It was the best time . . . . It would have been the best time, but . . . .

141

I went into the hall to find my coat on the hook. I pulled out the globe. "How can I tell about my lie?" I asked. I looked deep into the fizzy pink ball. I saw John Englehart in the ball. He was leaning over my shoulder.

"Why are you making wild-boar faces at me?" I asked.

"I wanted to make you laugh," he said. "And maybe it's my hair."

I took a good look. He was right.

I was so surprised I dropped the globe. The whole thing shattered into a million pieces. I looked down. Pink fizz was running along the floor. It smelt like strawberry pop. That's all it was. Strawberry pop.

I didn't have to believe in the globe. I just had to believe in myself.

Mrs. Holstein came out to see what the noise was and started to help me sweep up the mess. Before she could say one word I told her. "It wasn't a composition, it was a lie," I said. "I'm so sorry."

She thought about it for a moment. "Not good," she said.

"No," I said.

"But you'll write a new composition next week. This time you can really tell about ballet."

"Yes." I took a breath. I felt light. I felt as if I were up on my toes. I looked at John Englehart.

And then I thought of the scissors.

John Englehart didn't know it yet, but he wasn't going to be a wild boar much longer.

I took another breath. I darted and jumped ahead of him. It was time to begin ballet.

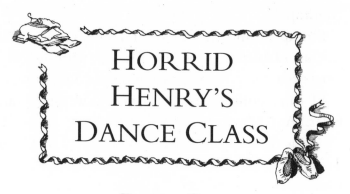

HORRID HENRY'S DANCE CLASS

Francesca Simon

Stomp Stomp Stomp Stomp Stomp Stomp Stomp.

Horrid Henry was practicing his elephant dance.

Tap Tap Tap Tap Tap Tap Tap.

Perfect Peter was practicing his raindrop dance.

Peter was practicing being a raindrop for his dance class show.

Henry was also supposed to be practicing being a raindrop.

But Henry did not want to be a raindrop. He did not want to be a tomato, a string bean, or a banana either.

Stomp Stomp Stomp went Henry's heavy boots.

Tap Tap Tap went Peter's tap shoes.

"You're doing it wrong, Henry," said Peter.

"No, I'm not," said Henry.

144

"You are too," said Peter. "We're supposed to be raindrops."

Stomp Stomp Stomp went Henry's boots. He was an elephant smashing his way through the jungle, trampling on everyone who stood in his way.

"I can't concentrate with you stomping," said Peter. "And I have to practice my solo."

"Who cares?" screamed Horrid Henry. "I hate dancing, I hate dance class, and most of all, I hate you!"

This was not entirely true. Horrid Henry loved dancing. Henry danced in his bedroom. Henry danced up and down the stairs. Henry danced on the new sofa and on the kitchen table.

What Henry hated was having to dance with other children.

"Couldn't I go to karate instead?" asked Henry every Saturday.

"No," said Mom. "Too violent."

"Judo?" said Henry.

"N–O spells no," said Dad.

So every Saturday morning at 9:45 A.M., Henry and Peter's father drove them to Miss Impatience Tutu's Dance Studio.

Miss Impatience Tutu was skinny and bony. She had long, stringy gray hair. Her nose was sharp. Her elbows were pointy. Her knees were knobbly. No one had ever seen her smile.

Perhaps this was because Impatience Tutu hated teaching.

Impatience Tutu hated noise.

Impatience Tutu hated children.

But most of all Impatience Tutu hated Horrid Henry.

This was not surprising. When Miss Tutu shouted, "Class, lift your left legs," eleven legs lifted. One right leg sagged to the floor.

When Miss Tutu screamed, "Heel, toe, heel, toe," eleven dainty feet tapped away. One clumpy foot stomped toe, heel, toe, heel.

When Miss Tutu bellowed, "Class, skip to your right," eleven bodies turned to the right. One body galumphed to the left.

Naturally, no one wanted to dance with Henry. Or indeed, anywhere near Henry. Today's class, unfortunately, was no different.

"Miss Tutu, Henry is treading on my toes," said Jeffrey.

"Miss Tutu, Henry is kicking my legs," said Linda.

"Miss Tutu, Henry is bumping me," said Camilla.

"HENRY!" screeched Miss Tutu.

"Yeah," said Henry.

"I am a patient woman, and you are trying my patience to the limit," hissed Miss Tutu. "Any more bad behavior and you will be very sorry."

"What will happen?" asked Horrid Henry eagerly.

Miss Tutu stood very tall. She took a long, bony finger and dragged it slowly across her throat.

Henry decided that he would rather live to do battle another day. He stood on the side, gnashing his teeth, pretending he was an enormous crocodile about to gobble up Miss Tutu.

"This is our final rehearsal before the show," barked Miss Tutu. "Everything must be perfect."

Eleven faces stared at Miss Tutu. One face scowled at the floor.

"Tomatoes and beans to the front," ordered Miss Tutu.

"When Miss Thumper plays the music everyone will stretch out their arms to the sky, to kiss the morning hello. Raindrops, stand at the back next to the giant green leaves and wait until the beans find the magic bananas. And Henry," spat Miss Tutu, glaring, "TRY to get it right."

"Positions, everybody. Miss Thumper, the opening music please!" shouted Miss Tutu.

Miss Thumper banged away.

The tomatoes weaved in and out, twirling.

The beans pirouetted.

The bananas pointed their toes and swayed.

The raindrops pitter-patted.

All except one. Henry waved his arms frantically and raced around the room. Then he crashed into the beans.

"HENRY!" screeched Miss Tutu.

"Yeah," scowled Henry.

"Sit in the corner!"

Henry was delighted. He sat in the corner and made horrible rude faces while Peter did his raindrop solo.

Tap tap tap tap tap tap tap. Tappa tappa tappa tappa tap tap tap. Tappa tip tappa tip tappa tappa tappa tip.

"Was that perfect, Miss Tutu?" asked Peter.

Miss Tutu sighed. "Perfect, Peter, as always," she said, and the corner of her mouth trembled slightly.

This was the closest Miss Tutu ever came to smiling.

Then she saw Henry slouching on the chair. Her mouth drooped back into its normal grim position.

Miss Tutu tugged Henry off the chair. She shoved him to the very back of the stage, behind the other raindrops. Then she pushed him behind a giant green leaf.

"Stand there!" shouted Miss Tutu.

"But no one will see me here," said Henry.

"Precisely," said Miss Tutu.

It was showtime.

The curtain was about to rise.

The children stood quietly on stage.

Perfect Peter was so excited he almost bounced up and down. Naturally, he controlled himself and stood still.

Horrid Henry was not very excited.

He did not want to be a raindrop.

And he certainly did not want to be a raindrop who danced behind a giant green leaf.

Miss Thumper waddled over to the piano. She banged on the keys.

The curtain went up.

Henry's mom and dad were in the audience with the other parents. As usual they sat in the back row, in case they had to make a quick getaway.

They smiled and waved at Peter, standing proudly at the front.

"Can you see Henry?" whispered Henry's mom.

Henry's dad squinted at the stage.

A tuft of red hair stuck up behind the green leaf.

"I think that's him behind the leaf," said his father doubtfully.

"I wonder why Henry is hiding," said Mom. "It's not like him to be shy."

"Hmmmn," said Dad.

"Shhh," hissed the parents beside them.

Henry watched the tomatoes and beans searching on tiptoe for the magic bananas.

I'm not staying back here, he thought, and pushed his way through the raindrops.

"Stop pushing, Henry!" hissed Linda.

Henry pushed harder, then did a few pitter-pats with the other raindrops.

Miss Tutu stretched out a bony arm and yanked Henry back behind the scenery.

Who wants to be a raindrop anyway, thought Henry. I can do what I like hidden here.

The tomatoes weaved in and out, twirling.

The beans pirouetted.

The bananas pointed their toes and swayed.

The raindrops pitter-patted.

Henry flapped his arms and pretended he was a pterodactyl about to pounce on Miss Tutu.

Round and round he flew, homing in on his prey.

Perfect Peter stepped to the front and began his solo.

Tap Tap Tap Tap Tap Tap—CRASH!

One giant green leaf fell on top of the raindrops, knocking them over.

The raindrops collided with the tomatoes.

The tomatoes smashed into the string beans.

The string beans bumped into the bananas.

Perfect Peter turned his head to see what was happening and danced off the stage into the front row.

Miss Tutu fainted.

The only person still standing on stage was Henry.

Stomp Stomp Stomp Stomp Stomp Stomp Stomp.

Henry did his elephant dance.

Boom Boom Boom Boom Boom Boom Boom.

Henry did his wild buffalo dance.

Peter tried to scramble back on stage.

The curtain fell.

There was a long silence, then Henry's parents clapped.

No one else did, so Henry's parents stopped.

All the other parents ran up to Miss Tutu and started shouting.

"I don't see why that horrid boy should have had such a long solo while all Linda did was lie on the floor," yelled one mother.

"My Jeffrey is a much better dancer than that boy," shouted another. "He should have done the solo."

"I didn't know you taught modern dance, Miss Tutu," said Camilla's mother. "Come, Camilla," she added, sweeping from the room.

"HENRY!!" screeched Miss Tutu. "Leave my dance studio at once!"

"Whoopee!" shouted Henry. He knew that next Saturday he would be at karate class at last.

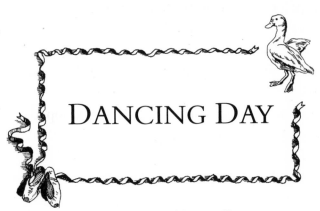

DANCING DAY

Robina Beckles Willson

Joanna put on her new red ballet shoes, and straight away she wanted to dance. She went dancing out of the house. She went dancing to her gate.

When Bill came by, she said to him, "Can I go with you? I can't go by myself. And I need to go dancing down the street."

"Oh all right," said Bill. "As long as I don't have to dance. I'm going to the park. And boys don't dance in football boots."

They said goodbye to Joanna's mother. And she went running into the house.

Joanna went running and skipping and dancing, all the way down the street. And Bill went after her kicking a stone.

"Boys don't ever dance like that. Can't you stop dancing?" he said to Joanna.

"I don't think I can. It must be my shoes. Because they are red. And because they are new."

As she went past some people, Bill saw them swaying.

"Why are they all swaying about?" he said.

Two tall policemen were walking slowly, side by side, along the street. But when they saw Joanna dancing . . . .

They started to bounce in their big black shoes. Bouncy bounce, then bump, bump, bump.

They turned to each other, and clicked with their fingers. Flicky flick, then click, click, click.

"Look at them," said Joanna. "Just like me."

"As bad as you," said Bill. "Boys don't dance like that. Come on. I am going to the park."

As they went past a busy shop, the ladies all swung their shopping bags. Swing swing swing.

And Joanna went dancing. Springy spring, then jump jump jump.

And the babies were clapping in their prams, as Joanna went dancing. Skippy skip, then hop hop hop.

"Come ON," said Bill. "Boys don't dance, you know, and I'm not dancing to the park."

When the flower seller saw Joanna dancing, she began waving her bunches of flowers. And Joanna went whirling and twirling around her.

Then the garbage truck came down the street. "Garbage men won't dance," said Bill, as they went thud with the garbage cans.

But, when they saw Joanna dancing . . . .

They banged their lids, and clicked with their heels. Bangy bang, then clonk clonk clonk.

"I tell you, boys don't dance," said Bill.

But then the dog behind him barked. And he began to dance to Bill. His tail went twirly twirl, then wag wag wag. And Bill found himself dancing in football boots.

Two cats joined in, with waving tails. Round him and round him, pad pad pad.

"Can't you stop them, Joanna?" he said as he bounded.

"I don't want to stop them. Come on to the park."

"But boys don't dance," said Bill.

And around the next corner they found the milkman. He saw Joanna, and started dancing.

At the park gate, the ice cream man began prancing. Whirly whirl, then spin spin spin.

"Perhaps boys dance a bit," said Bill.

The football boys all danced with Joanna. Bendy bend, then kick kick kick.

And the ducks came out of the water, just to dance with Bill. Floppy flop, then plonk plonk plonk.

"It's a special day in my new shoes," said Joanna.

"A dancing day, you mean," said Bill. "I think I'll dance, just for today."

So the boys and the ducks and the cats and the dog were dancing and prancing with Joanna and Bill, until it was time to go home to bed.

Acknowledgments

The publisher would like to thank the copyright holders for permission to reproduce the following copyright material:

Vivian French: the author for "Boys Don't Do Ballet—Do They?" Copyright © 1998 Vivian French. **Patricia Lee Gauch:** From *Bravo Tanya* by Patricia Lee Gauch. Copyright © 1992 by Patricia Lee Gauch. Used by permission of Philomel Books, a division of Penguin Putnam, Inc. **Patricia Reilly Giff:** Sterling Lord Literistic, Inc. for "Adele On Her Toes" by Patricia Reilly Giff. Copyright © 1998 Patricia Reilly Giff. **Gelsey Kirkland and Greg Lawrence:** "Rosie, the Little Ballerina" from *Little Ballerina and the Dancing Horse* by Gelsey Kirkland and Greg Lawrence. Copyright © 1993 by Gelsey Kirkland and Greg Lawrence. Illustrated by Jacqueline Rogers. Used by permission of Doubleday, a division of Bantam Doubleday Dell Publishing Group, Inc. **Margaret Mahy:** "The Hookywalker Dancers" from *The Door in the Air and Other Stories* by Margaret Mahy. Copyright © 1976, 1988 by Margaret Mahy. Illustrations copyright © 1988 by Diana Catchpole. Used by permission of Bantam Doubleday Dell Books for Young Readers. **Bel Mooney:** David Higham Associates Ltd. for "I Don't Want to Dance" by Bel Mooney from *Prima Ballerina*, edited by Miriam Hodgson, Methuen Children's Books 1992. Copyright © 1992 Bel Mooney. **Caroline Plaisted:** "A Tin of Sequins" copyright © 1998 Caroline Plaisted. **Alison Prince:** Jennifer Luithlen Agency for "The Dog Star" by Alison Prince. Copyright © 1998 Alison Prince. **Jean Richardson:** The author for *Out of Step*, J. M. Dent 1993. Copyright © Jean Richardson 1993, 1998. **Joan G. Robinson:** Penguin Books for "Teddy Robinson Goes to the Dancing Class" from *Teddy Robinson Himself* by Joan G. Robinson, George G. Harrap & Co. Ltd. 1957. Copyright © 1957 Joan G. Robinson. **Francesca Simon:** The Orion Publishing Group Ltd. for "Horrid Henry's Dance Class" from *Horrid Henry and Other Stories* by Francesca Simon, Orion Children's Books 1994. Copyright © 1994 Francesca Simon. **Penny Speller:** Laurence Pollinger Ltd. for "Anna's Shoes" by Penny Speller. Copyright © 1998 Penny Speller. **Jean Ure:** The Maggie Noach Literary Agency for "Silver Shoes" by Jean Ure. Copyright © 1998 Jean Ure. **Robina Beckles Willson:** A. M. Heath & Company Ltd. for *Dancing Day* by Robina Beckles Willson, Ernest Benn 1971. Copyright © Robina Beckles Willson.

Every effort has been made to obtain permission to reproduce copyright material but there may be cases where we have been unable to trace a copyright holder. The publisher will be happy to correct any omissions in future printings.